Shatt

Malcolm Jackson ha
he returned now
gunfighter. He hope
and his wife Betty
ter had struck dur
been murdered whi
falsely accused of k

The whole town
taken over by new
the air. Who was
have a crooked sh
ber?

It was down to
his brother's deat
was he man enoug

Shattering Guns

Zeke Martin

ROBERT HALE · LONDON

© Vic J. Hanson 1956, 2003
First hardcover edition 2003

ISBN 0 7090 7281 3

Robert Hale Limited
Clerkenwell House
Clerkenwell Green
London EC1R 0HT

The right of Vic J. Hanson to be
identified as author of this work has been
asserted by him in accordance with the Copyright,
Design and Patents Act 1988.

Typeset by
Derek Doyle & Associates, Liverpool.
Printed and bound in Great Britain by
Antony Rowe Limited, Wiltshire

CHAPTER I

The Kid saw the face in the bar-room window and recognized Joe Cater. The Kid raised his hand to wave but the face disappeared. The Kid almost reined in his horse and went to get himself a drink and say howdy to Joe. But he changed his mind. Home was what he had been looking forward to in all these weeks of a long and dusty trail and home still called, the call stronger than ever now.

The Kid's maw and paw were long since dead, shadows of a dim past, victims of the Indian Wars. Home meant brother Pete and his wife Lucy, and the two kids. Home meant the weather-beaten white frame house at the end of the main drag, the hammock on the wide porch, the apple tree sagging voluptuously over the porch roof.

He only had about a quarter of a mile to go now and he would be there. As a nipper he'd always thought the main drag of Pendant to be the longest in Kingdom Come. And it hadn't changed none: right now it seemed to stretch into infinity.

He saw an old-timer he used to know, though he couldn't remember the old buzzard's name. He opened his mouth to speak but the old man turned his head away. For a moment the Kid was puzzled but then he realized that, though the leathery old-timer hadn't changed much, he himself must have done. Hell, when he left Pendant he was an unwashed babe. But now . . . he shook his head as if to dispel his thoughts. Maybe he'd grown a little too fast, riding along Pendant main drag like a conquering hero coming home and expecting everybody to run out into the street and holler welcome.

There were very few folks around. People would be eating, or, at least, sheltering from the noonday sun. Puffs of dust awakened beneath the slow, steady clop-clop of his horse's hoofs as the beast picked its way gingerly among the cart-ruts.

No, the old place hadn't changed much. Shabby and run-down as all get-out, though maybe it had always been that way and he hadn't noticed it in the old days. The sun beat down on him but he was past feeling it now. The new togs he had bought before he started out were crumpled and dust-stained from his journey.

There was nothing striking about him, why would anybody notice him? He was just a young saddle-tramp with an empty belly and a head full of memories, riding down the main drag of a Western township which also had no claim to fame. It was his home-town but he had never liked it, had always looked upon it as a nasty mean kind of community. Had it changed at all? he wondered.

One thing he could be sure of, however, was that brother Pete wouldn't have changed. He would be as bluff and hearty as ever with a strong hand and a booming greeting for the kid brother. Some of Lucy's home cooking would go down well too. Buxom Lucy with the laughing eyes and brown-gold hair.

But the children would have changed. Kids never did stay put, they just grew and grew. The Kid wondered if Timmy and Arrabella would know him now. He gave his horse a reassuring pat as the beast stumbled a little in a particularly treacherous rut. The Kid could remember skinning his knees more than once in just such a rut in this very same street in the old days.

Hardly before he realized, so deep had he been

sunk in his reverie, he had reached his destination. There was the house right there in front of him. The front lawn was as brown and unkempt as ever. The decrepit boughs of the apple-tree rested plumb on the top of the sagging porch roof. The hammock was still there, though it looked a lot smaller than the Kid remembered it.

He dismounted from his horse and loped the reins over the picket fence. The gate squeaked protestingly as he opened it and as he strode up the gravelled path, windows seemed to watch him like so many sightless uncommunicative eyes. He knew Pete would be out at the ranch this time of day. He ramroded the Diamond K for that old skinflint Luke Price and worked like a railroad trojan.

The kid tried the front door and found it locked or stuck or something. He figured Lucy was round back. Maybe the kids were at school, did they still go to school he wondered. His scuffed high-heels clattered on the porch floor. The porch went right round the house, comfortable and cool after the sun. The Kid whistled shrilly. The back door opened at his touch.

Nothing was cooking in the kitchen. The place was spick and span. He hollered but there was no answer. He went through the house from room to room. The place was empty. Here and there it was a little dusty, which was strange, for Lucy had always been a houseproud wench.

The Kid figured maybe the family had gone on holiday someplace. Pete certainly worked hard enough. The Kid could never remember him having a holiday before. Maybe old Luke Price was getting generous in his old age. It was typical of Pete and Lucy that they'd left the back door unlocked, though petty housebreaking wasn't among the main faults of the townsfolk of Pendant.

The Kid left the house and crossed to the small stables. There was a little feed there but the cast-iron horse-trough was dry. He took a bucket and went over to the pump. He remembered how three bucketfuls had always filled the trough. He filled it and went and fetched his horse and unsaddled him and left him to his repast. Then he walked back down the main drag to the saloon.

He didn't pass anybody he knew. There was brooding stillness about Pendant. To the Kid it seemed to be an almost dangerous stillness, a *mean* stillness – though maybe that was just due to the oppressive heat. Rain was badly needed.

Joe Cater was behind his bar, standing facing the batwings, his hands placed downwards on the bar in front of him, his fat shoulders hunched. It was almost as if Joe had been waiting for the Kid. And the latter couldn't help wondering whether the saloon-keeper had indeed seen him from the window when he went past in the first place.

The bar-room was empty except for four men playing cards at a corner table. They looked up as the newcomer crossed the floor then turned back to their game. The Kid didn't think he knew any of them.

Joe Cater was fatter than ever, his bulbous eyes more prominent. His red face was frog-like as it slowly creased in a smile. The Kid had always thought Joe's smile was kind of false. It was falser than ever now. But the Kid knew Joe had recognized him and so he said, 'Howdy, old-timer,' with forced joviality and he knew he was the one being false now. Truth was, he had never really liked fat Joe Cater.

'Well, well, Mal!' Joe's voice boomed with hail-fellow-well-met.

At first something didn't quite click with the Kid. On the long and hard trails, round the chuck-waggon and in the hierarchy of the owlhoot he had been known and respected as 'The Kid'. No longer a boy but the Kid, the one and only Kid. In those years he had almost forgotten his own name. And that had been easy to do: he never had been able to figure what had got into his folks when they dubbed him Malcolm. It made him sound like a cissy English dude or something.

He bellied up to the bar and Joe asked him to name his pizen and he chose rye. 'Have one with me, Joe,' he said. He winked and reached under the bar. 'Special,' he said as he produced the bottle. He turned and got two glasses. 'We'll make the first two on the house, Mal,' he said.

His movements were smooth for all his bulk. Fast, too, professional. The Kid knew that Joe would be as fast too with the loaded shotgun he always kept under the bar. Joe was smiling all the time, the fixed professional smile he had for everybody. Like a Cheshire Cat with lockjaw. Some people called him Happy Joe. They were usually people who didn't know him very well. Joe smiled because it was good business, because it pleased the suckers, because it fooled the troublemaker and threw him off his guard.

But the Kid was neither a sucker or a troublemaker. Nobody could possibly have taken him for either of these things. And so Joe's smile slowly faded and, watching him, the Kid realized that Joe had hardly been aware that he was smiling at all and the expression he wore now was his natural one.

It was as if Joe's face was off-guard. His blubber sagged unhealthily and the Kid realized that Joe was getting old. Joe's face wore a lugubrious expression, a worried one. Even, maybe, an expression that had in it a hint of nameless fear. And as the Kid watched this face now, scrutinized it from under lowered hatbrim the way a good gunfighter would do, he began to experience a sense of disquiet, a first hint of anxiety.

But he hid his thoughts and returned Joe's mechanical good wishes and downed his drink. Then he slipped a coin on the bar and said: 'My turn now.'

Joe refilled the glasses. The Kid took a sip of the second drink then looked straight at the saloon-man. But his voice was casual when he said:

'I've just been down to Pete's. There's nobody there. D'yuh know whether they've gone away or sump'n?'

Joe's head jerked up, his frog-like eyes seemed to be starting from his head. But he looked down again quickly, giving the Kid a view of a bald tonsure. Joe seemed to be trying to find the answers to questions in the depths of his brimming glass.

Finally he said, 'Miss Lucy an' the kids are out at Ma Brannigan's place.'

He took a drink quickly but still did not meet the Kid's eyes. His hands were flat on the bar again as if he was bracing himself to prevent his blubber from quivering. But still it came: the inevitable question: 'So where's Pete?' asked the younger man.

This was a new Mal. No longer a boy. Joe had seen the new Mal coming through the batwings like a young leopard; he bore the stamp of a gunfighter. And now the picture was complete as Joe looked up fleetingly again and saw the eyes gone suddenly cold, heard the voice, toneless, almost menacing, brooking no argument.

'Bad news, Mal,' mumbled Joe.

'If anything's happened to Pete I want to know about it,' said the toneless voice. 'Tell me, Joe. Where's Pete? What's happened to him?'

Joe steeled himself to meet those eyes but couldn't keep the fear out of his own eyes now. Naked fear. He looked like a man surrounded by fear and now the Kid was just another fear to pile on top of the others. And the Kid realized it must be something pretty bad to make tough, jolly Joe Cater that afraid.

'Pete's dead,' said Joe.

But the Kid had guessed that already. 'How did he die?' he asked.

'About three weeks ago.'

'I didn't say when, I said how?' The voice was implacable.

Joe blurted the words out. 'He was shot – in the back.'

There was silence for a moment. Then the cold voice spoke again. 'You saw me ride in didn't you, Joe?'

'Yes, Mal.'

'I guess other folks did too, but they pretended not to.'

'I guess none of them wanted to be the one to tell you.' Joe's voice was easier now, but he was still wary.

The inevitable question came: 'Who did it, Joe?'

The saloon-keeper's words came out in a spurt. 'Pete was in jail. He bust loose. He was shot while trying to escape in the dark . . .'

The voice tailed off. Joe shut his lips tightly. He had said all he meant to say. The Kid seemed to realize this. He was silent for a moment, then he said suddenly:

'First thing I got to do is go see Lucy I guess.' Next moment he was crossing the batwings. He didn't even say 'so-long'.

Joe waited till his footsteps had almost faded then came out from behind the bar and crossed to the window. Mal had moved fast. There was no sign of him now.

Joe knew the eyes of the card-players were on him. Presently he went back behind the bar. The men forgot about him, concentrated on their game. But Joe waited a while longer before taking off his white apron and slipping out the back way.

CHAPTER II

Ma Brannigan's little spread where Lucy and the kids were staying was a few miles out of town.

What had Joe been scared of, wondered the Kid as he rode. Before he left town he had seen another man he knew. The fella had made no sign of greeting, had dodged into a nearby emporium with what had seemed unusual alacrity.

Wouldn't anybody talk unless he buttonholed them the way he had buttonholed Joe, stuck there behind his bar like a fat frog?

The Kid set his horse at a gallop, working out his grief, his rage and his frustration in speed.

Only when he topped a rise and looked down at the peaceful valley with the Brannigan place like a toy in the centre of it did he slow down.

He gentled his horse down the slope. The ranch, though spick and span as ever, looked deserted and he was reminded of that other place back in town, the motionless curtains, the dust on the furniture. But he shook the thoughts away from him. Most ranch-buildings looked deserted this time of day when the hands were out on the range.

He passed the corral, swerved his horse to the left to approach the ranch-house. The low one-storey bunkhouse was to the right of him, drowsing in the sun like some long brown animal. Between the bunkhouse and the two-storey ranch house was a large barn. It was from the shadows of this that the figure suddenly appeared.

The Kid squinted his eyes against the sun-glare and instinctively dropped his hand. But he halted the movement, froze. A sensible man didn't make funny moves when he was covered by a sawn-off shotgun. They could blow a hole in you as wide as a gate.

The figure was a slight one in jeans and a battered wideawake. It came nearer. The shotgun was elevated a little. If the trigger was squeezed now the Kid figured the charge would just about take his head off. He stared at the muzzle of the gun and, as it moved nearer, the face above it. Only then did he realize the newcomer was a girl.

At first he could hardly believe his eyes.

He found his voice. 'Betty Lou!'

The brown face puckered. Then the shotgun

muzzle slowly tipped and the girl said: 'And you're Mal Jackson.'

He dismounted slowly, still wary until she ground the butt of the shotgun in the sod. He saw now that the jeans fitted her the way they could fit no man. And the white shirt-waist too. And, despite her efforts to make it otherwise the thick taffy hair tumbled from beneath the shabby man's hat.

She was looking up at him now and her eyes were clear and blue, her chin firm, a strong-boned boyish face that held all the beauty of womanhood too. He could hardly believe that this was the freckled awkward creature he had teased as a kid, but he knew it must be so.

They were both silent, busy with their own thoughts as she led the way.

Ma Brannigan came out onto the veranda. She was a big rawboned woman with iron-grey hair. Her clothes were mannish, except for her homespun skirt. On her feet were Indian moccasins, a change from her usual riding-boots. She had evidently been busy around the house.

She greeted him soberly but with welcome. She stepped aside to let him enter the house and then he saw Lucy half hidden in the shadows of the doorway. His sister-in-law came forward. She had changed. She looked much, much older.

'Mal!' she said. 'Mal . . .' Next moment she was sobbing in his arms.

He patted her shoulders and tried to murmur soothing words. He wasn't good at this. Her ravaged face was hidden from him now but he could see the streaks of grey in her dark hair.

Ma took charge and ushered them all into the house. And there, after they had had a meal, it was Ma who told the story. Lucy sat in the shadows.

It had all started with the rustling. All the spreads around Pendant had lost cattle. Ma Brannigan had been hit a couple of times. The bigger spreads had suffered more, including the Diamond K where Mal's brother had been ramrod. The thieves came and went like ghosts, leaving not hide nor hair of a clue.

Riding the Diamond K range one day Pete Jackson had surprised a bunch of strange riders using a running-iron on beef. They had shot his horse and escaped. He gave the alarm then rounded up another horse and took the trail.

His boss, old Luke Price, and a bunch of his riders weren't far behind Pete but they lost sight of him. They followed his trail to a low range of hills just outside the Diamond K boundary. There a shot from ambush pitched old Luke dying from his horse.

Old Luke never spoke again. Two of the riders took him back to the ranch. The rest went on but were not fired at again. It seemed as if the bushwhacker had chosen the rancher for his target and, after doing that job, was content. The riders came across Pete on foot in the hills. He said his horse had stumbled in a cleft, thrown him and bolted. But Pete still carried his Winchester and it was proved subsequently that it was a bullet from this rifle that had killed Luke.

No trace was found of the rustlers Pete Jackson claimed to have seen, neither could the riders find trace of the rustlers' fire where they had used a running-iron on stolen critturs.

The sheriff took over, indicted Pete for the murder of Luke Price. Motive: Luke was a childless widower and in his will, drawn up by a Pendant lawyer barely two weeks before the crime, he had left the Diamond K and all its stock to his *segunda*, Pete Jackson. The law alleged that Pete had made up a cock-and-bull story about rustlers so he could get Luke out on the range, bushwhack him and blame it on the thieves.

Pete, denying everything, was asked how it came about that a bullet from his rifle had killed Luke. Pete said he had lost his rifle when the rustlers shot his horse. Afterwards, on his second trip out, he had heard the shot and rode in the direction of the sound. He had found his rifle among the rocks. One shell had been fired. There was nobody around.

'All Pete's old friends stood by him, of course,' said Ma. 'But things looked mighty strange to people who didn't know Pete the way we did. The sheriff had to lock him up.'

'But Sheriff Pinson knew Pete,' burst out the Kid. 'He knows . . .'

'It wasn't Kurt Pinson,' said Ma. 'He's retired, gone back East to live with his daughter. We've got a new sheriff, a younger man, named George Corletta.'

'Never heard of him,' said the Kid.

'He's kind of a fancy-pants. Used to be a Texas Ranger – good at his job though – he works hard.'

'Was it him who shot Pete?'

'Nobody knows who shot Pete. He picked the lock of his cell door with a knife a well-wisher must've got to him somehow. He didn't get far before the sheriff found the cell empty and gave the alarm. Pete was coming out of the livery stables on a horse when somebody shot him in the back in the dark. Nobody knows who did it. There was a mob there in no time: if the killer had left any traces they were soon trampled down.'

The story was almost finished. Lucy, speaking at last, told the final part. She was almost hidden in the shadows of her corner. The day was getting long in the dusk. It would soon be dark.

It was a pitiful little tale, this aftermath of the larger, tragic story. The attitude of the people in town changed towards Lucy and the children. They became to be treated almost as pariahs.

'Narrow-minded, ignorant dogs,' snapped Ma Brannigan. 'Tuppenny counter-jumpers and scrub-cutters.'

'Well, if somebody intended to scare us away from town, they certainly succeeded,' said Lucy. 'I'd've been scared for the kids all the time.'

'I told her she ought to be at the Diamond K,' said Ma Brannigan. 'It's hers by right now.'

'In town they say not,' said Lucy. 'Even Lawyer Kramer ain't sure. I want no more trouble for my children.'

'Where are the kids now?' asked the Kid. 'Surely they don't still go to the school in Pendant.'

'No, I send 'em to Jamestown. They go with Bill Jacoby's two kids. Their old negro man, Mose, takes them and fetches them in the trap every day. They should be back any time now. Nobody knows them in Jamestown. It's a bigger and better school there, too. Bill Jacoby and his two boys are good friends of all of us . . .'

Lucy's voice tailed away. Ma Brannigan said, 'Me an' Betty Lou get all our groceries in Jamestown now. We seldom go near Pendant. The place is evil. Particularly since that new bunch of carpet-baggers moved in and started to take things over.'

The Kid leaned forward in his chair. 'What new bunch, Ma? The sheriff maybe . . . and are there others?'

'Well, I dunno, not the sheriff maybe,' said Ma. 'He turned up before the others. The main one I'm thinking of is Burt Hopson. He calls himself a Southern gentleman. He blew into town about six months ago and took over Papa Pablo's cantina. Have you seen the cantina since you came home, Mal?'

'No, I didn't pass that way.'

'You probably wouldn't have recognized it anyway. Hopson had an extra wing tacked onto it. It's a restaurant, gambling-hall, gin-palace and dance-hall combined. Quite a hell-hole by all acounts – girls an' all. Hopson was on his own to begin with. Him an' his money-belt. He bought the cantina an' Papa Pablo went back to Mexico. Then Hopson bought the Loop Triangle spread too.'

'What made Mike Ramsgate sell the Loop Triangle?' put in the Kid.

'Mike's bin dead some time. Got trampled in a stampede. After that his missus hated the sight of the place. She was glad to sell out. She advertised in the papers. I guess that's how Burt Hopson got to know about it. He changed the ranch a whole lot too, had a whole herd of workmen out. Then when everything was fixed out here as well as in town, he started to bring in his hands, his gamblers, his girls. Trouble-shooters, gunslingers . . .'

Ma made an abrupt gesture with her mannish hands. The Kid's lips quirked a little in his brown poker-face. He wondered what Ma had thought of him when she first saw him again. Did he too, bear the stamp of the gunslinger?

He had heard pretty much everything he needed for the time being. He rose. Ma said:

'You're goin' to bunk down here ain't yuh, Mal?'

'Thanks, Ma,' he said. 'You know I'd like to, but I think mebbe town 'ud be the best place for me. I can keep closer to things there.'

Betty Lou went out with him and helped him to saddle up, held the horse's bridle as he mounted. She looked up at him.

'Lucy wasn't being morbid, Mal,' she said. 'You must take care.'

He bent and kissed her lightly on the cheek. It

had seemed natural for him to do so. Just a brotherly peck; but her hand was in his for a moment before he went away.

CHAPTER III

The Kid found Papa Pablo's cantina easily enough. The place, now night was here, seemed to be the hub of the town. It no longer looked like Papa Pablo's place.

The old cantina was still there but it had had an extra floor built atop it and a garish false front, complete with naptha flares to boot. The name was changed. A huge white board was painted in black and gold lettering: THE GOLDEN CALF.

The name had a strange effect on the Kid. It awakened echoes in his mind. Memories of childhood that had brought him pleasure but now only brought him sadness because Pete was irrevocably tied up with those memories. The Golden Calf: there was a biblical ring about it . . . the schoolhouse on the hill (it had been smaller then), the old teacher with the grey beard (long since dead) who had seemed like God himself. It seemed to the Kid there was something hypocritical and blasphemous about the name, The Golden Calf. Cold rage filled him again, so that, as he shouldered through the batwings he was ripe for anything.

He was met by a blast of hot air, redolent with the stink of unwashed humanity, cheap scent, tobacco-smoke. Blue smoke hung around the crystal chandeliers; somewhere a band was playing; among the babble a girl squealed. Folks turned to look at the Kid, turned away again. There were so many of his kind in Pendant nowadays; lean young men who looked to be as much on a hair-trigger as their guns undoubtedly were.

The Kid made a bee-line for the ornate mirrors at the far end of the room. There, no doubt, lay the bar. He was no respector of persons and, in his present mood, as dangerous as a mountain-cat. He went through the crowd without deviating and folks gave way before him. That way he drew more attention to himself, but that didn't seem to faze him none. One man, thrust roughly aside, turned menacingly. He met the gaze of the Kid's cold eyes and subsided, muttering.

The Kid elbowed his way to the long bar, pressed his lean belly against it. There were two barmen. A fat man and a lean one with a scarred face. The Kid crooked a finger at the latter and ordered a double-rye.

'Howdy, Mal,' said a voice at his elbow.

The kid turned, recognized the newcomer as an old school-friend of his.

'Hallo, Jim,' he said. He became interested. Jim and he had always been friends. Maybe Jim would be able to tell him more about Pete's death.

But Jim didn't have a chance: before he could speak again, another voice beat him to it.

'So this is Pete Jackson's brother. I heard he was in town.'

The voice had a jeering undertone. The Kid turned slowly, elbow on the bar, to look at the speaker. The thought passed through his mind that somebody hadn't wasted much time. He exchanged glances with a bulky black-jowled man with a prize-fighter's face and only one eye.

'This is Randy Kane, Mal,' said Jim. 'We call him One-eye.' He gave a spurt of nervous laughter.

'Howdy,' said the Kid. He held out his hand, waited for One-eye's next move.

He heard movement all around him and knew that people were withdrawing from that area of the bar. His old friend, Jim, didn't seem quite so near either.

'I won't shake hands with the brother of a filthy bushwhacker,' said One-eye.

The Kid raised his eyebrows, giving his poker-face an unwonted, almost ludicrous expression. He noticed that One-eye's hand was very near to his low-slung gun. For all his bulk, the skunk was probably fast: pugs usually were.

The Kid looked at the rejected hand in surprise. The hand flicked upwards, out. The back of it smacked against One-eye's blubbery lips with a mushy sound. It was followed by the contents of the Kid's glass, flung with the other hand. One-eye staggered, cursing and spluttering. He tripped over the brass footrail at the base of the bar and sprawled on his back. His slouch hat rolled at the Kid's feet. The Kid kicked it negligently to one side.

Using the bar as a lever, One-eye began to haul himself to his feet. The Kid moved a little way from the bar, his hands dangling loosely at his sides. He took a step nearer to One-eye.

One-eye lurched upright. In the same moment he went for his gun. Somewhere in the crowd a woman cried out, a sharp harsh sound. One-eye was fast. The Kid's draw was just a mite faster. He lunged forward; the barrel of his swinging gun bit into One-eye's wrist. One-eye howled with surprise and pain. His iron clattered to the floor at his feet.

With a smooth kind of follow-through movement, the Kid holstered his own gun. Then he got to work with his fists.

A left in One-eye's stomach, a bunched right in One-eye's already bleeding mouth. One-eye went back against the bar; a bottle fell over with a crash. The Kid's attack was savage, cruel. One-eye didn't have a chance to use any of the craft he had learned in the ring. He was demoralized; his fists flailed. One of them found a mark on the Kid's shoulder, spinning him around. But the younger man was as light on his feet as a dancer. The blow only seemed to give him added momentum.

It increased his savagery too. He was no longer poker-faced. His slate-blue eyes blazed, his lips were drawn back from strong white teeth. He pinned One-eye against the bar and slashed him to pieces with cruel, scientific blows.

Yes, the Kid knew how to fight too. But this was no longer a fight. It was cold-blooded mayhem. One-eye, the town bully, had picked himself a wild one. But not till the big man was a crumpled bloodstained bulk draped over the footrail did his punishment finish.

The Kid leaned back against the bar. He was panting. The colour came slowly back to his passion-filled face. The flames went out of his eyes. They became cold again as his gaze slowly swept the room. Only those near to him realized that he was trembling. But they had sense enough to know that it wasn't fright made him that way.

There were movements from different parts of the room. Movements, strangely enough, in both directions. Some people were going out. But others were moving up slowly, in devious directions, towards the bar. One-eye's pals, Burt Hopson's tough roustabouts, were moving in for the kill.

If the Kid noticed this he didn't show his awareness of the fact. He brushed a stray lock of hair from his eyes. He bent and picked up his hat and placed it carefully at just the right angle on his head. Beside him, One-eye groaned hollowly.

The Kid did a surprising thing then. He got down on his haunches by One-eye. The bruiser peered up at him, licked swollen lips. The Kid said in a clear loud voice:

'I could've killed you. Next time I will . . . And that goes for anybody else who slanders my brother's name.'

This fool kid was really sticking his neck out! Who did he think he was? A hellion all right, yeh. But did he think he was some kind of a superman too?

He had his back to the bar again now and the tough boys were closing in on him. He couldn't help but see them. They were all out in front of the mob. Frisco Dan, Lafe Pill, Obadiah Small, Bruiser Jenkins, Piute Mack . . .

But they pulled up short when they found themselves covered by the Kid's gun. 'The next man who moves gets a slug in the belly.'

The shuffling footsteps had ceased. A voice rang out. 'I don't think such a measure will be necessary.'

All eyes but those of the Kid and his foes were turned up to the balcony.

'You can put the gun away, younker,' went on the voice. 'My men won't molest you. If you don't put your gun away I'll have to shoot it out of your hand.'

The five hardcases were looking up at the balcony now. The Kid holstered his gun, pushed back his hat.

The other man began to come down the stairs. He had holstered his gun too.

They watched each other until they were face to face. 'Welcome to my place, Mr Jackson. I am Burt Hopson.'

The man was as supple as a greased whip. His face was strong, his lips thin and firm beneath the gambler's moustache, his eyes keen. His jacket was open and, slung below his speckled fancy waistcoat was a loaded gunbelt. His gun was pearl-handled, crouched in a beautiful tooled-leather holster.

Nothing there was purely for ornamentation, however. The holster was cut back for the fastest draw possible. The gun was a heavy Colt, a fancier edition of the Kid's own. But it hung low and the pouch was tied to Burt Hopson's thigh by a whang-string also the same type as the Kid's, the stripe of the gunfighter.

With a wave of his hand Burt Hopson said: 'A couple of you carry this carcase outside.' A negligent jerk of his head in the direction of the moaning One-eye. 'And dump it under the pump.'

Frisco Dan and Bruiser Jenkins came forward. They picked One-eye up and carried him away. With rather puzzled glances in their boss's direction, the other three bruisers brought up the rear of the cavalcade.

Burt Hopson joined the Kid at the bar. 'Have a drink with me, Mr Jackson.'

The Kid figured he could play this deadly dude at his own game. He made a graceful inclination of his head. 'Thank you, Mr Hopson.'

The saloon-cum-ranch-owner adopted a conspiratorial look. He had a lean handsome mobile face. 'I've got some special stuff I think you'll like.'

The lean scar-faced barman stood attentively

before them. Hopson leaned forward and spoke to him quietly.

'Yeh, boss.' The man scuttled along the bar, disappeared through a small door.

In a few moments he returned, brushing dust reverently from a long bottle with his white cloth. He opened the bottle carefully, served the pale amber liquid up in balloon-shaped glasses the like of which the Kid had not seen before.

'Fine old brandy,' said Hopson, and smacked his lips slightly.

The Kid tried it and had to admit it was good, plenty good.

'You handled One-eye like he's never been handled before,' said Hopson. 'It was a pleasure to watch. It was time the man was taken down a peg or two. He's a witless bully.'

Witless or not, reflected the Kid, One-eye had worked fast. He wondered if Hopson had sicked his tame bully onto him just to test his (the Kid's) ability.

'You're the kind of man I need,' said Hopson. 'You're fast and rough but you're not witless.'

'I hire my gun out to no man.'

Hopson chuckled as he poured out two more glasses of brandy. 'But you're staying in town I take it?'

'I think so.'

'Have you a place to stay?'

'Nope. Not yet.'

'We can find you a room in my establishment if you wish. Clean – and plenty of good food if you want it.'

'Thanks.'

George Corletta, Sheriff of Pendant, was only just past thirty but his thick brown hair was winged with grey over his ears and lines were irrevocably etched into the forehead and cheeks of his well-cut face.

He called 'Come in' to the knock on his office-door. He rose and came around the desk and held out his hand.

'I heard about you, Mr Jackson. You certainly made a mess of One-eye.'

'I did my best,' said the Kid and wasted no more time.

'I want you to tell me about my brother,' he said bluntly.

The sheriff said: 'I thought you would've heard it all by now. I can't tell you much more than anybody else. I had to arrest your brother. The evidence was pretty damning against him. I had to arrest him for his own good too: feeling ran pretty high in town.'

'Riff-raff,' spat the Kid. 'And you judged him

guilty like they did?'

'It is not my place to judge,' said the sheriff. 'I merely did my duty.' There was no pomposity in his voice.

'Where were you when he was shot?' asked the Kid.

Corletta seemed to weigh his words well before, after a short interval, he spoke.

'I had a good deputy when I first took this job. But his horse threw him. Busted his neck. He was an ex-wrangler. What a finish for a man who had spent most of his life in the saddle. I haven't had a deputy since. That's why, on the night I had your brother here, I was alone. I keep a Mexican boy here to do my fetchin' and carryin' for me but he was laid up with croup. I went down the street a piece to get me a cup of coffee and some pie . . .'

'Where did you go?'

'I went to Papa Pablo's.'

'But by that time it had become Burt Hopson's place . . .'

'Ye-eh. But he hadn't yet renamed it.'

Sheriff Corletta was not easily riled it seemed: even by curt questions that were shot at him with machine-gun-like rapidity. His face did not change expression. His voice continued evenly:

'I locked the office up behind me. I made sure the back was locked too . . .'

The Kid interrupted again, 'If, as you said a few minutes ago, feeling ran pretty high in town, wasn't it rather unwise to leave your prisoner alone?'

'The town had quietened down, gone back to its drinking an' gambling an' wenching. The area round here, round the jail, was as quiet as a tomb. I didn't think then that it was unwise to leave my prisoner alone. I've realized since that it was; but well . . .' The sheriff gave a little shrug.

'Mind you,' he went on, 'I figured that if a gang had decided to come and take the prisoner they'd wait till the middle of the night when all the law-abiding folks in Pendant were abed. I was ready for a long vigil. I aimed to sit up all night. I needed sustenance. That's why I went out. As a matter of fact, I aimed to bring something back here, both for myself and the prisoner. But I was forestalled. Things began to happen . . .'

The Kid had to hand it to this lawman, he certainly had a glib tongue.

'Somebody came into the cantina,' went on Corletta . . . 'yelling that Pete Jackson had bust out of the jail. I was running up the street when I heard the shot. But I was only one of the mob, a good many people got to the stables before I did. Pete was lying on his face just outside the stable door. He must've been leading a horse out when he was shot. The horse had bolted but somebody caught it . . .'

'An' Pete had been shot in the back.'

'Yes, an' nobody knew who had done it. There were no clues.'

'If Pete was leaving the stable when he was shot in the back, it figures his killer could've been hiding somewhere in the back of the stable . . .'

'I thought of that. I searched the stables but didn't find a thing. Of course, he could've been facing in another direction. He might even of been backing out of the stable as he led the horse, if the horse happened to be a skittish crittur. It figures then, that his killer was somebody outside who saw him escaping and took a pot-shot at him and then was ashamed to admit it.'

'Where was the hostler at the time?'

'He'd gone to get his supper.'

Everybody seemed to be conveniently missing when the job was done, reflected the Kid grimly. But this time he kept his mouth shut. He didn't aim to show all his cards to this gun-toting prairie lawyer. Not that he had a helluva lot of cards to play. Still, many a time he had backed things when he had a whole deck of pasteboards stacked dead against him. He rose to go. The sheriff rose too, came around the desk once more and shook hands with him. The Kid knew those muddy eyes

– with their tortured depths – were giving him a last once-over.

He called next at the livery stable and was lucky enough to meet the hostler who admitted to swigging coffee (also in Papa Pablo's) on the night Pete Jackson stole a horse and got himself bushwhacked. The hostler was a shifty-looking character with a hare-lip; but he didn't look as if he had enough savvy to figure out any kind of bushwhack frame. Unless somebody else had told him just what to do. If the Kid began to believe that this was indeed the case, he aimed to get rough. Until then he decided to take a leaf out of the sheriff's book and act friendly. The sorrowing brother retracing the last steps of Pete Jackson's life.

The hostler wasn't very helpful. The Kid choked back an impulse to pistol-whip the surly skunk until he sang, but bade him quite an affable 'So-long' instead.

The Kid went out into the morning sunshine. Though the hostler had been surly, which was obviously his nature, nobody, with the exception of One-eye, had been markedly unfriendly. The room he had occupied last night in The Golden Calf had been clean and comfortable. In fact, the bed, to one accustomed to sleeping on the range or on hard bunkhouse pallets, had been almost too comfortable. He had overslept and now it was late noon and he still had not completed all the chores he had promised himself for the morning.

He decided to have some chow before continuing his peregrinations; so he retraced his steps to The Golden Calf (formerly Papa Pablo's cantina) and entered the cantina proper. This had changed little from the old days, except that it had been renovated a little. The small half-circular zinc-covered bar was still there for the dispensing of drinks as well as eats. Behind the bar was the service-hatch and the door to the kitchen. The tables were still the same well-worn round ones in two sizes. The wooden chairs, though they might not have been the same ones, at least looked the same, strictly utilitarian.

There was no grizzled Papa Pablo behind the bar, however, but a fat man with a bald head and a bad-tempered expression. The Kid took a seat at one of the smaller tables designed for two diners. It was empty and in a corner. The Kid had his back to the wall and could survey the whole of the cantina. His was the true gunfighter's caution.

He knew people were looking him over. The man who had half-crippled One-eye. The brother of Pete Jackson, killer.

His old friend, Jim, who had beat such a hasty retreat when One-eye started to cut up rough last night, nodded a little sheepishly from the other side of the room. There were others the Kid knew, but, strangely enough, each one of them seemed to be either studiously immersed in a meal or looking in the other direction.

He saw, grouped at two tables close together in a corner, the five plug-uglies who but for the timely intervention of their boss, Burt Hopson, he would have tangled with last night. They had their heads together and didn't seem to be looking towards the new arrival either. Whether the baldheaded gink behind the bar knew the newcomer's identity or not the Kid couldn't be sure. But the baldheaded worthy was studiously looking in the other direction too.

The Kid took out his gun and felt, almost as much as heard, the rustle go through the room. This was followed by dead silence when the Kid hammered on the table-top with the butt of the gun, the sound was like a rolling clap of thunder.

The barman turned slowly as if he was being pulled on an invisible string. The Kid spun his gun nonchalantly by the trigger-guard. 'Let's have a leetle service over here, friend,' he called.

'Yes, sir.' The barman grabbed his white cloth, scuttled around the bar and made a sidling motion towards the Kid. The latter slowly holstered his gun. Something that sounded like a huge sigh rose up in the room. The diners went back to their meals.

After his dinner, which proved to be good after all, the Kid left the cantina and sought out the office of Lawyer Kramer.

The latter turned out to be a dried-up rat-like little man with no teeth or hair and bright pugnacious eyes. Mal Jackson didn't remember him and he didn't remember Mal. But, when the latter introduced himself and, in his forthright way, stated the purpose of his business the little rat became very pompous and legal.

But he was cut short. 'I thought that in this country a man is presumed innocent until he is proven guilty.' The Kid preened himself: he, too, could give out with the high-sounding phrases if need be.

Lawyer Kramer decided that, despite his youth, this Jackson buck was a sharp one. 'Yes-um. But this is a strange case. In all my handling of wills and bequests I have never come across a case like it before. Much study and investigation is needed . . .'

'One of those slick high-priced Eastern lawyers could fix it I guess.'

The lawyer had nothing to say to this. 'Couldn't they?' the Kid pressed.

Thus pinned down, Lawyer Kramer said, 'Um – yes. I suppose so.'

'Get one then. I'll give you three days. That ought to be plenty of time to get one here. Get a good one. And don't worry about the expense.'

'Um – ye-es . . .' But the Kid was already on the way out.

CHAPTER IV

The dying sun etched purple shadows on the blood-red slopes of the hill. The shadows were the shadows of crosses on the humps over which the wind blustered endlessly as it tried to find its way to the town in the dip below.

The shadowy half-time between light and darkness, when the dying sun was like a gout of blood, was hardly the time to be visiting such a spot. But that fact did not seem to be worrying the lone figure who stood now amid the wind-blown desolation.

Away in the hills a coyote howled and the Kid raised his head. Standing here over his brother's grave he had been living for a moment in the past. Pete had been a good brother and Mal, the black sheep of the family, had not always appreciated this fact.

Now, before turning away Mal made a solemn vow and then he retraced his steps down the hill to the frame house that had once been his home.

It was quiet at this end of town. Darkness fell quickly. The Kid thought he heard footsteps behind him and he stopped.

He turned. Then the shot in the darkness made him whirl again.

He fell into a crouch, the gun-butt warm and comforting in the palm of his hand. His thumb rested gently on the hammer. The muzzle was already tilted clear of the cut-down top of the holster.

There was no more sound. But the shot had come quite near. Still half-crouching, he moved silently on.

The man lay on his face just past the corner of the house-fence. Even in the darkness the Kid could see the slowly-widening patch of blood between the shoulder blades. He rolled the body over and looked into the dead, contorted face of Randy Kane – known as One-eye.

He saw the gun too, lying a couple of feet away from the body. He holstered his own gun and picked up this one and spun the chambers and discovered that one slug had been fired.

Suddenly he realised what he had walked into, but by that time it was too late. Even as he began to turn the voice behind him said:

'Drop the gun, killer, an' put up your hands.'

The Kid let his gun thud to the ground and raised his hands above his head.

The voice said: 'Go take his gun, Frisco. Then run an' fetch the sheriff while I keep him covered.'

Frisco came around the Kid and picked up the gun. Everything, it seemed, had been figured to a nicety.

Frisco's heavy footsteps shuffled away down the street. The sound faded. Frisco's unseen pard said, 'Don't try any funny tricks, killer, or I'll blow a hole in the back of your neck.'

The Kid lay on the bunk in the two by four 'dobe cell and listened to the ominous sounds from down the street. He was conserving his strength. Unless those hooligans outside were just playing up for the hell of it he figured that pretty soon he'd need plenty of stamina. He was not easily scared; he felt helpless, frustrated. But he had heard that sound before; if he didn't miss his guess this was the real thing.

He remembered vividly the terrible end of an old saddle-pard, Little Micki Santos. Micki had knifed a man in a saloon brawl in a town in Kansas where there seemed to be an inordinate amount of prejudice against Mexicans. The Law had clapped him in jail and, only an hour after, the lynch-mob had come. Micki's three pards, which included the Kid, had tried to stop things. They had pointed out that the dead townsman had been an unprepossessing character who cheated at cards and was little loss to the community. But they might as well have been blowing against the wind, they were swept aside by the blood-lusting mob. Micki, battered and reviled, died kicking at the end of a rope.

. . . The Kid came to himself with a start when the human wolves howled more loudly from outside . . . And he could still remember the way Micki had looked swinging on the night-winds from the bough of that tree like a sodden bundle of rags.

The Kid began to sweat. He rose from the bunk and went over to the cell-door and shook it and yelled, 'Sheriff, what's going on out there? Sheriff . . .'

George Corletta came through the door between the office and the cell-block. He had a gun in his hand and he didn't come close to the barred door. Under the yellow light there was a film of sweat on his brow.

'What's going on out there?' the Kid asked again. But he wasn't shouting now; his eyes stared through the bars with cold contemptuous fury.

'The boys are just whooping it up I guess,' said the sheriff.

'They're coming closer,' the Kid told him. 'I've heard that sound before. They're telling each other what hell-for-leather riproaring characters they are. They might be coming here pretty soon to try and prove it.'

'I can handle them,' said the sheriff and turned away.

The Kid called after him, 'You better let me out of here an' give me a gun.'

But it didn't work. The door closed – but softly – behind the lawman.

The Kid cursed under his breath. He turned and recrossed the cell. He climbed onto the bunk and peered through the bars of the small window. This looked out on an alley. The Kid couldn't see a thing but blackness – *blankness*.

But the sounds came to him more clearly, turning his blood cold.

Isolated voices rose now and then above the general babble. The Kid could not distinguish any words but there was a note of triumph about those voices. Now the Kid could hear the tramp of feet, too, and the voices, blending together, sounded like the baying of blood-hungry wolves.

Maybe the gang out front had also got people planted out back too, ready to blast him if he tried to make a getaway. Fat chance . . . he was penned here like a sitting duck, helpless, impotent. Once more he grabbed the bars of the door and rattled and yelled for the sheriff. Then it was almost as if the mob out front heard him: they roared: the Kid knew now that they were right outside the door.

The Kid had only ever heard the sea once in his life. That was when his peregrinations had taken him to the coast of California. A plainsman born and bred, the sea had unsettled him. The sound of it had got on his nerves. Now he remembered the sound it had made one night during a raging storm and he lay on a flea-ridden bunk in a stinking doss-house and listened and tried to sleep. The sound coming from outside was like the sound he had heard that night, ravening, all-powerful, bloodlusting.

Suddenly, a single voice rose above the rest. 'Open the door, sheriff, or we'll break it down!'

George Corletta shouted something in reply but his words were drowned by the cries of others in the crowd as they backed up their spokesman. Again the hopelessness of the Kid's position overwhelmed him and he ran to the bars of his door and yelled with rage and frustration. As if to echo his fury the place vibrated again under blows from a battering-ram, a cacaphony of sound which dinned his ears and drowned the sound of his own voice. The Kid became blind with fury, he wanted to get to grips with the mob, to tear into them, to attack them with hands, feet, teeth, everything he had.

The communicating door opened, bringing more sound with it, devilish sound.

The sheriff stood there, his gun in one hand, his keys in the other.

The Kid cursed him savagely, vilely, and finished up by commanding him to open the cell-door. Like a man in a trance, the sheriff came forward. His face gleamed with sweat. His eyes looked old, old . . .

He waved his gun recklessly. 'Get back,' he cried in an unnaturally hoarse voice. 'Back!'

The Kid backed slowly away from the bars. 'Let me out of here, you crazy freak,' he said.

The sheriff unlocked the door and swung it open. His gun was levelled in front of him as he retreated to his office door. The building shook again with the impact of the battering-ram on the outer door. Wood splintered and groaned agonizingly.

'I'm giving you a chance to make a run for it out back!' yelled Sheriff George Corletta.

The Kid came out of the cell. 'Give me a gun,' he said.

'I can't chance it,' said the sheriff. 'You might

turn it on me.' He jerked his gun. 'Go on, get moving. You haven't got much time.'

The Kid turned away from him, moved swiftly towards the back door.

The building shook as if in the midst of a hurricane. Voices screamed and hollered. The Kid's thoughts were chaotic as he turned the key in the back door and eased it open a tiny crack.

He couldn't help remembering the movement out here in the blackness that he thought he had seen when he peered from his cell window. Had it been some kind of an optical illusion after all or was he due to walk into a hail of hot lead? Or maybe he was just slated for a bullet in the back the way his brother Pete had gotten his!

As he opened the door a little wider his body was tensed.

The darkness closed in around him. The free breeze was on his face, rustling his hair, but his flesh was contracting, anticipating the bite of hot slugs.

A voice said his name and he whirled, his hand going instinctively to his hip. But there was no gun there, not even a holster.

'Mal, it's Ma Brannigan.'

He could not believe his ears. But then they were all around him and a hand grabbed his arm and he was led through the darkness. He began to see things then. He saw that it was indeed Ma who had hold of his arm and she had men with her who were fanning out to protect him on all sides. He almost stumbled over something on the ground.

'That's the skunk who was waiting out here to bushwhack yuh,' said Ma.

The Kid came to his senses. 'Maybe we ought to take him along,' he said. 'Maybe there're a few things he could tell us.'

'You've got something there, Mal,' said Ma in her mannish tones.

She left him for a moment, moved among the men. Two of them went back to the recumbent man. They grabbed a leg apiece and dragged the insensible bulk along the hard-packed ground.

Out front the hounds were still baying. The Kid wondered whether they had busted into the jail yet. For a moment too, he wondered how the sheriff would fare when the mob discovered the bird had flown. Somehow he didn't figure the sheriff would come to much harm. He couldn't figure that character at all somehow.

Ma's coup had been well-organized. Horses were waiting and a spare one for the Kid. He insisted on having the prisoner on the front of his saddle, so he could gloat over him, he said. He did not waste his breath in spouting thanks for his deliverance, knowing that it would only embarrass his rescuers, particularly Ma, who had a heart of gold beneath her hard shell.

CHAPTER V

As they rode, the Kid, his eyes now more accustomed to the darkness, began to recognize some of the men around him. There was Ma's foreman, Curly Randle, and two more of Ma's boys. But the other four, the Kid was surprised to see, were old Luke Price hands from the Diamond K. He couldn't quite figure why these boys should elect to rescue the brother of the man alleged to have killed their boss. Although, on the other hand . . . these had been Pete's friends. Tall, cadaverous, Grat Boyce; pudgy Len Mallin; pint-size Ben Druge; and the mulatto boy, Mortimer Jaques.

Ma told him that it was Morty Jaques who had taken to the Diamond K the news of the Kid's arrest. These four boys had ridden straightaway to Ma's spread and a little rescue party had been formed.

'A frame-up, uh?' said Ma.

'Not a doubt,' said the Kid. 'But I'm still trying to figure out how far the frame-up was supposed to go. What I mean is – was the mob all worked out beforehand and did the mob mean to go through with it or was the sheriff meant to act scared and let me go so that this skunk . . .' he indicated the still bulk across the front of his saddle . . . 'could pick me off. We're purty near Ranger country here. It'd sound better for a prisoner to be shot escaping than be finished by a lynch-mob who'd dragged him out of the jail. The Rangers have a nasty habit of taking a lynch-town apart to see what makes it tick so nastily.'

'You think mebbe the sheriff was in the plot all along?' said Ma.

'I dunno. I hardly know what to think.'

'The sheriff's kind of a sad sort of gink,' said Ma. 'He used to be a Ranger y'know.'

'So I heard,' said the Kid drily. To Ma the word 'Ranger' seemed to be synonymous with integrity and straight dealing. But the Kid had known some Rangers in his time, good ones and bad ones. He had been on both sides of the fence. The Rangers were a tough bunch of characters; they gave no quarter and they expected none. Many of them were what you might call dedicated men. The Kid couldn't help wondering why George Corletta, still a comparatively young man and good officer material had left the Rangers and taken up a lawman's post in a stinking little burg like Pendant.

The mulatto boy, Morty Jaques, had joined in the conversation. He said that the lynch-mob had gathered, not in The Golden Calf as one might have imagined, but in Joe Cater's saloon.

'But there were a lot of Burt Hopson's men there,' said Morty. 'And the ringleader was One-eye's pard, Lafe Pill.'

All these names were becoming more familiar to the Kid. He said: 'Frisco Dan and Bruiser Perkins picked me up. Lafe Pill led the lynch-mob. Could be there's the fine hand of Burt Hopson somewhere in this, uh?'

'It's a distinct possibility,' said Ma Brannigan drily.

'But it seems strange that the mob met in Joe Cater's place instead of The Golden Calf,' said the Kid.

Ma said: 'Oh, I dunno. Burt Hopson bought up Joe's place you know.'

'Is that a fact?'

'Yeh, Joe's just a manager now. But maybe Hopson figured it wouldn't look quite so blatant if the mob started from Joe's place instead of his own.'

'Somebody must want me out of the way pretty bad,' said the Kid. 'Maybe they're scared I might find out too much.' There was no hint of *braggadocio* about his words. He knew his own capabilities and realized that, despite his youth, other people must recognize them too.

There was silence for a while, a silence broken only by the thudding of hoofs, the creak of leather, the jingle of harness. There had, as yet, been no sounds of pursuit. Could be that the rescue party had gotten clean away. If so, by now the lynch-mob must be wondering whether their prospective victim had vanished into thin air and their tame bushwhacker with him.

The Kid suddenly realized that they weren't making for Ma's spread. He realized too that this was well, as Ma's spread would be the first place a posse would look for him.

'Where are we going, Ma?' he asked.

'The Diamond K,' said Ma.

The Kid was surprised. 'I don't see how . . .'

Ma cut him short. 'Let it rest, Mal. Let it rest. We'll go into it all when we get there.'

The Kid let it rest. Anything for Ma. Hadn't she stuck her neck out for him? And, even if she hadn't . . . well, Ma was Ma and a man just didn't gainsay her.

He changed the subject, poked a hand into the recumbent bulk before him. 'He's sleeping soundly. I hope the skunk ain't dead.' The Kid grabbed the man's hair and lifted his head, twisted it. The hair was gummy with blood, the face blotched with it. 'Looks a mite sick. But I think he's still breathing.'

The miles rolled away beneath the horses' hoofs, bringing them nearer every moment to their destination. Yes, the Kid hoped the man was going to live. He aimed to be quite ruthless with the skunk. If the skunk wanted to keep on living he better start spilling the beans as soon as he woke up.

The Diamond K was reached. 'We don't reckon the law 'ud look for you here,' said Ma.

The Kid had to agree with her on that. But he kept his mouth shut. Lights were on, their yellow rays streaming out across the corral. There was a welcoming air about the place. The Kid might almost have been coming home, really coming home.

Ma said, 'Me an' Curly an' the boys will have to be going now to see that Lucy and the kids are all right. If the law is going to pay us a visit we want to be at home before it gets there.'

'I ought to be there,' expostulated the Kid. 'If they come I . . .'

'Don't fret, Mal,' put in Ma's foreman, Curly Randle. 'Me an' the boys'll be along. We can handle ourselves.'

The Kid had to admit that Curly and his

bobcats could handle pretty well anything. So he let it go.

He watched Ma and the boys till they disappeared into the darkness. Then he helped Len Mallin to carry the still unconscious bushwhacker into the bunkhouse. Here under the yellow light more of the late Luke Price's Diamond K hands waited. They all greeted the Kid, though, here and there, with a little restraint. The Kid figured this was only natural: he didn't let it faze him none.

The bushwhacker was laid on an unblanketed bunk. There was a swelling broken welt, encrusted with dried blood, on his forehead. 'He's still alive,' said pudgy Len Mallin. 'But he's in a bad way. May be he's got concussion or something. You certainly hit him an almighty wallop, Grat.'

Grat said: 'Leave the skunk be. He'll keep. I guess he'll last out till we want him . . .' He raised his voice. 'Hey, Fats, where's that damned coffee?'

The fat cook bustled in carrying a tray piled with mugs of steaming brown liquid. He threw a 'howdy' in the general direction of Mal Jackson, planked the tray on the deal table, and retreated. He reappeared again a few moments later with another tray, this time of hot cookies.

The Kid drew his chair up with the others. The coffee was good. So were the cookies. He replenished his stamina. This was one time he waited for somebody else to take the initiative.

Finally Grat Boyce began to speak. 'First of all, Mal,' he said, 'We want you to know how bad we feel about the way your brother died. If you look around you, you'll realize that all the men in this bunkhouse are old Diamond K hands. Real old hands I mean – not one of us had been with old Luke under five years. Most of us have been here over ten. You brother, Pete, was our friend . . .'

The Kid became reckless then. 'All right then, why did . . .'

Grat held up a large lean hand. 'Wait. We know what you aim to say. Maybe you'll let Mort tell it now. He was the only one of us there when old Luke was shot.'

This puzzled the Kid, but he turned towards the mulatto ranny and waited.

Mortimer Jaques' dark, earnest face was set. He said: 'When Pete come running in and said thieves wuz using a running-iron on our beef there was only me and four more hands at the ranch. All the rest of the boys, including everybody here, were out riding someplace. Us five had chores to do around the corral an' barns, that's why we happened to be here. The other four men were new hands. Old Luke had only set 'em on a couple of weeks before, he was enlarging all the while y'know, taking on new stock. He needed new hands.

'Pete got himself a hoss right off an' left us. Ol' Luke led the five of us after him. You know what happened next. I gotta admit that things looked bad for Pete when we caught him with that rifle an' the one shell gone. But I never figured Pete had done it: I knew Pete too well. It was the others. They wuz four to one. They took Pete into town. I went along – I figured the sheriff would see sense. But the sheriff's a newcomer too . . .' Mort spread his hands in an eloquent gesture.

Grat Boyce said: 'If the trial had come off I think they'd have had a job to pin old Luke's killing on Pete. His escape an' the shooting were very convenient.'

'A frame?' spat the Kid.

Grat nodded. 'Yes. We weren't sure at first, but we're sure now – after what's happened tonight. They wanted to fix you too, so you wouldn't dig too deep.'

The Kid turned once more to the coloured ranny. 'What happened to those other four men, Mort?'

'They weren't very popular here. They're working for Burt Hopson now.'

'Maybe they were working for Hopson all along,' said the Kid. 'Who were they?'

Mort ticked them off on his fingers as he named them.

'Frisco Dan, Bruiser Jenkins, Jay Davies, Lemmy Banks...'

'The first two I've met,' said the Kid grimly. 'They're the two who so conveniently found me by the body of One-eye an' handed me over to the sheriff. They're died-in-the-wool Hopson boys all right. The other two I never heard of.'

'I misinformed you I guess,' said Mort gravely. 'The other two you don't have to worry about. They wuz saddle-pards just the way Frisco an' Bruiser are saddlepards. Jay Davies got kilt in a gunfight an' his pard, Lemm Banks, lit out an' ain't bin heerd of sence.'

'Wal, that narrows things down a bit anyway,' said the Kid. 'Now we're gettin' someplace. All in all, I've got a mighty big score to settle with Frisco Dan an' Bruiser Jenkins. And the sooner the better.'

The prisoner in the bunk groaned hollowly. The men left the table and gathered around him.

Ma Brannigan and her boys reached the spread without mishap. They dismounted at the corral and right away the staunch old frontierswoman began to give out once more with the orders. With Curly adding his two-cents worth, the men dispersed in all directions, melted silently into the shadows. Ma went on to the ranchhouse, where a deputation awaited her.

This consisted of her daughter, Betty Lou, and her guests, Lucy Jackson and the two kids, Timmy and Arrabella. The two last-named, from whom no secrets could be kept, had insisted on staying up until they learned how Ma and the boys had fared in their daring coup.

Blonde and well set up, Timmy a head taller than his sister, the two of them dashed forward. The two young women behind them, the brown-haired widow and the taffy-haired daughter, waited motionless. This moment was fraught with anxiety.

But it was an anxiety that Ma soon dispelled as she waved a big hand and boomed, 'Nothin' to it. Nary a scratch. We weren't even seen.'

'Mal . . .' Lucy and Betty Lou cried the name in unison and looked at each other in surprise.

Betty Lou was thankful that the darkness hid her blushes. It was natural that Lucy should be anxious about her one-and-only brother-in-law; but need she (Betty Lou) have acted so eager? But, even so, her breath was short, quick, as she awaited her mother's reply.

'He's at the Diamond K. Whole an' sweet as a nut. An' a fine bunch of boys to back him up if anything goes wrong.'

Ma grabbed Timmy and Arrabella each by the scruff of the neck and propelled them onto the veranda.

'Ma Brannigan, did anybody get killed?' carolled Timmy.

'No, you bloodthirsty young Cheyenne. C'mon, off to bed with you, both of you, or I'll take your scalps an' use 'em for dish-clouts.'

The two kids shrieked with glee. Ma's blood-curdling threats were a constant source of amusement to them. Goodnight kisses were exchanged all round and off they went.

'I'm as hungry as a timber-wolf,' said Ma. 'You got anything in the pot, Betty Lou?'

'Sure thing, Ma.' Betty Lou was as gay as a bird.

Ma was halfway through her second dish of stew when the sound of hammering hoofs came from outside, getting steadily louder.

Ma rose, grabbed her gunbelt and buckled it around her ample waist. The other women rose too.

'You stay here,' said Ma.

'We're coming with you,' said Betty Lou.

'You'll stay here,' said Ma. 'Whose gonna watch the kids, see they don't come down? Grab a gun apiece if you like, though I don't think you'll need 'em.'

Whether the two girls shared Ma's gusty optimism was doubtful, but they had to admit she was rigid in the other respect. Betty Lou got the two spare guns out of the dresser drawer, handed Lucy one. Then the two of them followed Ma to the door, but no further. They watched her cross the veranda, go down the steps.

Beyond her there was light; a strange light. Ma's bulky form was limmed against it as she marched towards the corral, one hand hooked in her belt, like a gunslinger going out to meet his foe.

The atmosphere of the humdrum little ranch was suddenly strange, almost eerie.

The hammering of hoofbeats was reaching a crescendo. Curly had done his job well. Along the corral fence, where it faced out onto the range, a row of torches had been placed and lit. And, as Ma had figured, the blood-crazy posse was making right for the ranch without let-up. They must've figured the lights were a camp or something – maybe somebody had caught their fox for them and wanted to make mighty sure that they wouldn't miss him.

The mob was well in the range of the yellow lights before Sheriff Corletta, his hand in the air, managed to stop it. And even then some of the riders, carried on by their own momentum, shot past him, milled around him.

Curly's voice rang out. 'All right. Stay right there, all of yuh, or we'll start shooting!'

Curly and his men were spaced out in and around the corral. All of them were in some kind of cover, behind barrels, barrows, old carts and other of the miscellaneous odds and ends that tend to gather around ranch-buildings. Each one had a rifle or shotgun levelled at the riders. The latter had piled up into a tight-packed bunch. One blast of firing could cut a swathe through them as wide as a covered wagon.

Ma strode across the corral.

There was something fearless and elemental about this woman which awed the mob. Collectively, it collapsed like a pricked balloon.

Ma was utterly fearless. She almost annihilated the mob by her offhand manner. Despite her bulk she climbed the fence like a five-year-old and sat on the other side, facing the mob.

There was silence now, broken only by the soughing of the wind and the occasional creaking of saddle-leather and the clinking of harness.

Ma's voice rang out. 'What's eating you people? We thought we were being attacked by a horde of rustlers aiming to carry the whole caboodle off.'

Behind Ma, one of her boys tittered. There was a rustle in front of her, almost a sheepish rustle.

Then the sheriff's voice rang out.

'This is a posse, Ma Brannigan. We're . . .'

'Rather large for a posse ain't it?' interrupted Ma.

'Citizens! They want justice. They want to catch a murderer.'

'What murderer?'

'Mal Jackson has escaped. He was helped to escape.'

'Who helped him?'

For a moment the sheriff was nonplussed. And his voice was less arrogant when he said, 'We wish we knew.'

'Well, Mal's not here, if that's what you think,' said Ma.

But this time it wasn't the sheriff who took up the gauntlet but somebody behind him. A voice yelled, 'We aim to search the place anyway.'

Some of Ma's boys recognized the voice of Frisco Dan. Curly in fact, made a mental note to blow Dan's guts out one day, if somebody else didn't beat him to it.

'You're gonna get hurt if you try,' retorted Ma.

'This is the law, Ma Brannigan,' said the sheriff.

'What, all of it?'

'Yes, if you want it that way. In a case like this a lawman has the right to . . .'

'I'll tell you what I'll do,' interrupted Ma. She straddled her legs, her hands pressed to her ample thighs. 'I've always been a believer in law an' order an' peace an' all. So, I'll let the law come in an' search. You, sheriff, an' one other man. The rest of you will stay put.'

'I can't make . . .'

'Scared?' jeered Ma.

So the sheriff's manhood was in dispute. Finally, accompanied by another man, he rode forward. The other man was one of the townsfolk, a storeman who had bolstered up his courage. It was noticeable that neither Frisco Dan or any of his ilk came forward: with their vicious tortuous minds, they suspected some kind of a trap.

Ma climbed down from her perch and led the way. With the two men in tow she disappeared beyond the range of the torchlight. The two opposing sides faced each other across the corral. Just shapes in the darkness, here and there the white blob of a face, the light glinting on the barrel of a gun. The members of the 'posse' grumbled among themselves. Frisco Dan's voice rose truculently from time to time. But Curly and his men remained silent, and all the more menacing.

The Kid and his friends of the Diamond K didn't seem to be having much luck with their prisoner.

He mumbled in delirium: nothing he said made sense. The Kid and Grat Boyce – who had dealt the terrible blow which had laid the man out – had sat up all night. Now, as the morning sunshine streamed through the dusty windows of the bunkhouse, they slept. The fat cook took over. During the recent troubles (only by a seeming miracle had a range-war been averted) he had had experience with all kinds of wounds and the succour and nursing of battered men.

But he couldn't do a thing with this character. He pronounced, 'By the look of him he oughta be dead.'

'Mal an' Grat ain't gonna be pleased,' said another man.

But the bushwhacker died anyway and the Kid and the foreman were acquainted with the fact as soon as they awakened.

The Kid swore with fervour and versatility. 'Jumping Jesophat!' exclaimed one admiring cowpoke. 'Where in tarnation did you learn such fancy cursing?'

'Bury him,' said Grat laconically. He meant the bushwhacker.

This was done. The Kid rose. 'As soon as I've had some chow I aim to go an' see how Ma and the rest got on last night.'

'You'll be shoving your neck plumb into a

noose,' Grat told him. 'I'll wager that the sheriff's men or Hopson's men, or both, will be watching the place an' keeping out of sight. They'll be waiting for you to turn up. Morty Jaques has gone over there to fetch a saddle horse that Ma promised us. Nobody'll suspect Mort of being mixed-up with your escape, particularly when he brings the horse back. He ought to be here soon.'

Before the two men had finished their belated breakfast, the coloured ranny did indeed turn up.

'The skunks followed me quite a piece,' he said. 'But they didn't come near enough for me to recognize any of them.'

'How're Ma an' the folks?' asked the Kid impatiently.

'They're fine. Just fine.' Mort's dusty face split into an oversized grin.

With many embellishments he told of how the 'posse' had been buffaloed. And not a shot fired either, though it had been a close thing.

Everybody chortled. 'Curly was particularly disappointed,' spluttered Morty. 'He wanted Frisco Dan's scalp.'

'An' he ain't the only one,' said the Kid.

He added. 'I reckon I'll ride over and see Ma after dusk anyway.'

This time even Grat Boyce did not argue with him. The men carried on with the work in the usual way. At intervals one or two of them rode in off the range. They reported that everything was quiet. There were no strange riders lurking around. Evidently the Pendant hardcases did not suspect the Diamond K of having had anything to do with the escape of Mal Jackson, the Kid.

CHAPTER VI

That night there was no moon. The stars were high too, so that what little light they gave was of a pale eerie quality, playing tricks with the landscape, giving it a shifting quality, so that a man could imagine there was an enemy behind every tree, every rock, in every pool of shadow, beyond every rise.

The Kid, beating a sweeping route to Ma Brannigan's place, was as taut and watchful as a mountain cat. He rode his horse at a steady lope, one hand gently holding the reins, the other on his thigh, close to the butt of his gun or, alternatively, the rifle in its saddle-scabbard. He rode upright in the saddle but with shoulders drooped a little, ready for a quick draw, or a dive for cover if need be.

The route he was taking led through more cover than the direct trail from the Diamond K to

Ma's place. But the hunter could use cover just as much as the hunted, as the Kid was pretty soon to find out.

He was approaching a small outcrop of rocks, nebulous in the eerie starlight, when his horse whinnied. The Kid swung sideways in the saddle and the slug which was aimed at him passed through empty air. The Kid's Colt was in his hand: he thumbed the hammer and the blatter of his shots was like the rolling echoes of the last rifle shot from his enemy.

He sent a blistering hail of lead at the outcrop, pinning the man down there: hoping there was only one of 'em anyway. Meanwhile he reached up and grabbed his own rifle from its scabbard. If there was only one man there the Kid knew he had to get him quick, before his pardners, probably within listening distance, heard the shots and came a-running.

The Kid was furious, reckless. He dived under the horse's belly and, rifle in one hand, revolver in the other, made a crouching zig-zag dash for the outcrop of rocks.

This crazy move took the bushwhacker completely by surprise. Next moment the Kid was at the rocks, leaping over them.

There was only one man and he crouched in a hollow. The Kid's rush carried him literally on top of the man. They were so close that neither of them had a chance to use their guns again.

The bushwhacker's rifle was skittled from his hand and clattered onto the rocks. The Kid's Colt went the same way. He decided he didn't need his rifle anyway, so he dropped it behind him. If this character wanted a hand-to-hand combat, the Kid was his man. Probably the bushwhacker hadn't wanted it this way at all. It was thrust upon him with a vengeance; but he did not run away from it.

His swarthy unshaven face was demoniacal; his eyes blazed into the Kid's, full of the desire to rend and tear this cocky young upstart who dared rifle-bullets and twisted and spat like a wildcat. He was a bulky, muscular man. He had weight on his side and he made full use of it. He had evidently had some experience of the 'mill', no-holds-barred to boot.

He fought with nails, teeth, elbows, feet. The two men rolled and scratched and grunted like a couple of wildcats. They had not much room. They scrambled among the rocks while the pale stars looked down on them in unwinking wonder.

To the fighters the world was black and topsy-turvy, shot with red stabs of passion and pain. A knee ground into the side of the Kid's head, giving him a kaleidoscopic vision of stars far more numerous and brilliant than the real ones. He struck back savagely, instinctively, a gust of primitive jubilation spurting through him as he felt his fists strike home on flesh and bones.

He scrabbled upwards, rose to his knees. The other man straightened and the Kid measured him and struck another blow. But the bushwhacker was tough and willing. He rocked and came back for more. In their ludicrous positions, on their knees like suppliants who had paused in their praying to squabble, they swapped blows.

The bushwhacker was the heaviest; he packed some pile-drivers. But the Kid was the fastest, the most supple, and the pile-drivers did not land or, at least, lost their power on a moving target. The Kid's torso and head were as if they belonged to a swaying, bobbing Aunt Sally at the shooting-range of a county fair.

A particularly bad miss sent the bushwhacker off balance and the Kid slammed him full in the teeth, sending him back so savagely that it seemed as if he would break off at the waist. But he was still very tough, with indiarubber qualities too, and when he bounced back there was a knife in his hand. He had become tired of playing handball and aimed to clinch things for keeps.

His first thrust tore a piece of cloth out of the Kid's shirt. Then they were up close, straining and grunting, and the darkness was alive with a murderous fury that made the stars blanch.

For a moment there was almost silence as the two men were locked almost immovably in mortal combat. Then there was an animal scream and one man broke away from the other and crumpled in a quiet heap.

In his old Indian fighting days the Kid might have taken his enemy's scalp as a trophy of victory. But now he was in a more 'civilized' country, he reflected sardonically, perhaps it was best he should not do such a thing. So he wiped the bloody steel on the dead man's shirt and tossed the knife away from him.

He found the man's rifle and Colt and inspected them by starlight. He decided neither of them were as good as his own weapons and might serve to incriminate him if he stole them. So he smashed them against the rocks, so they wouldn't be any use to anyone else, and tossed them into the maw of the night. They thudded to the ground; and then there was silence again, broken only by the sighing dirge of the wind.

He found the bushwhacker's horse finally, ground-hitched some distance away. He smacked it across the flank, sending it galloping away towards Pendant. Then he collected his weapons and remounted his own horse and continued on his journey. If the bushwhacker wasn't found by sunrise the buzzards would be glad of his presence.

The Kid completed his journey without further mishap. He was challenged from the darkness at the back of the Brannigan spread and sang out his identity. Curly Randle and another man came forward to greet him then let him pass through. Light blazed in the kitchen a second before the Kid knocked on the back door. It was opened by Betty Lou.

The light gushed out onto his face, making him blink. He stepped forward.

'Mal!' The cry was glad but a little choked. Next moment she was in his arms.

His body carried her backwards a little. He had the presence of mind to heel the door shut behind him. Then his lips found hers.

A gruff cough brought them to their senses. They parted, turned hand in hand to face Ma Brannigan. If the old dame objected to having a trouble-shooter as a prospective son-in-law she didn't show it. She beamed upon them. Right then she wouldn't have seemed at all out of character had she burbled, 'Bless you, my children.'

But she didn't. She jerked her head back and bellowed. 'Lucy! Kids! Mal's here!'

By tacit agreement Mal and Betty Lou separated completely now. The former went forward to meet the glad – and in Lucy's case a little tearful – onrush of the other three people.

He was amazed at the way the two kids had grown. Timmy was almost as big as Mal himself and Arrabella was filling out, would pretty soon be a beautiful young lady like Betty Lou.

The Kid, hard-boiled though he was, suddenly felt a little choked. If ever he wanted a home in the old territory this, it seemed, was it. Everybody was a little full-up. There was an embarrassed silence. This was broken by Betty Lou. Bright-eyed, pink-cheeked, she exclaimed, 'You're just in time, Mal. I was just going to fix something before the kids went to bed.'

'I'll help you,' said Ma. 'Take yourselves off, the rest of you. Make yourselves comfortable in the other room.'

The meal was worth the short wait. What had started out to be a snack finished up – in honour of the Kid – as a man-sized ranch supper. Eggs, sunny side up; prime ham; chip potatoes with batter; hot wheatcakes and maple syrup; cold apple pie and coffee with a dash of rum.

Afterwards the Kid leaned back with a bloated sigh of satisfaction. He loosened the top two buttons of his pants then took out his 'makings' and rolled himself a quirly. He blew smoke-rings for the edification of the ladies. Timmy pretended to be very blasé about it all: he would probably have been far more interested to see Uncle Mal doing tricks with the gun which hung in its belt over the back of a chair.

The Kid felt he could sit like this forever, lapped around by warmth and love. But he knew he mustn't get too complacently comfortable or in addition, he told himself sternly, too soft. He had man's work to do. Dark mean work. He figured he'd leave as soon as Arrabella and Timmy had gone to bed.

This was finally gotten over with. Arrabella left the imprint of a kiss on Uncle Mal's cheek. Then the Kid rose and buckled on his gunbelt.

'Where are you aiming for now, Mal?' asked Ma.

'Aw, just reconnoitring,' said the Kid airily.

The two women said nothing and, indeed, all three of them seemed to realize now that it would be useless to question him further. Betty Lou went out to his horse with him. They kissed again.

'Be careful, Mal,' she whispered.

'I will, *chiquita*.' He waved once before disappearing into the darkness.

He set his horse at a lope, going away from the back of the ranch. Then he began to make a wide detour, almost at a walking pace.

Pendant looked better by night. But the Kid

wasn't fooled by its spurious glitter. He had seen too many such places, held in the thrall of lawlessness, camouflaged beneath a cloak of respectability.

He steered his horse through a dark alley. Then in the pitch blackness of a clump of cottonwoods at the back of Pendant's main street he tethered the beast and left him.

He moved catlike through the darkness, his hand on the butt of his gun. He eased open the back door of Joe Cater's place. He paused to get his eyes accustomed to the new consistency of woolly darkness, then, after a moment, went on again.

The blare of voices, the occasional screech of a female, the clackety-clack of a decrepit piano came to him more clearly now. He found a door, opened it. He struck a match and looked about him, realizing he was in Joe's office. He crossed to the window and pulled down the blind. Then he lit the lamp and began to go through the drawers of the desk. These were singularly unproductive. Evidently Joe didn't keep many business records. Probably everything of that kind was now taken care of for him over at The Golden Calf.

Disgustedly, the Kid blew out the lamp. He went on along the passage until another door barred his way. He eased it open a fraction and the sounds of revelry came to him more forcibly.

He applied his eye to the crack and saw the broad back of Joe Cater. He took out his gun. He could've plugged Joe there and then, probably without the shot being heard.

But the Kid waited a while and his patience was rewarded. Joe turned presently and stepped towards the door and the Kid pressed himself against the wall behind it. Joe left the door open behind him. In the gush of light that came through, the Kid watched the man open the door of his office and disappear inside. The Kid eased the door to with his foot, cutting off the light. Then he, too, went along to the office door from under which a thread of yellow light already showed.

Joe was moving about inside; Kid heard the clink of glass. Gun in hand, he kicked the door open.

The bottle Joe had been holding slid from his fingers and shattered on the floor. The smell of raw hooch smote the air like a living fist. The jigger of whisky that Joe had poured remained untouched on the desk before him. Joe's face looked bloated. It was almost green beneath the light. His eyes bugged from his head.

'What's the matter, Joe?' asked the Kid. 'You scared I might tell your new boss you hide in the back to drink his liquor.' Already he could see the beads of sweat beginning to break out on the man's forehead beneath the yellow light.

Joe managed a sickly grin. 'W – What are you doin' here, Mal?'

'Just a little social call, Joe. I'd like a pow-wow with you.'

'Sure, Mat. B – but there's no need for the gun.'

'I think mebbe there is.' The Kid heeled the door to behind him. Then he went on remorselessly, 'I want to know who was responsible for the death of my brother. I want chapter and verse. I want to know who framed me, who engineered the lynch-mob . . .'

'I know nothing about . . .'

'The mob met in your place, not in The Golden Calf.'

'I couldn't help that. They just came. There was nothing I could do. If I had argued with 'em they would've tore the place to pieces – an' me with it maybe.' Joe's face became animated, the fear began to die from his eyes as he improvised on his story, kidding himself along.

'I don't really know how it started. One moment they were just kind of enjoying themselves, the next they were rampaging loco, yelling for your blood . . .'

'Who were the ringleaders?'

'Wal, I dunno, Mal. It was purty hard to tell in all that mob. They weren't just all the tough boys either – some of the old townsfolk were yelling loudest o' the lot . . .'

Joe's voice died off in an incoherent murmur.

'The townspeople were always a treacherous bloody-minded bunch,' said the Kid, huskily. 'There isn't a single one of 'em I can remember bein' really fond of.

'Come to think of it,' he added. 'I never did like *you*, Joe. Even as a kid I allus thought it'd be a good thing to kick you in your fat bloodsucking gut . . .'

'Mal! I . . .'

'Have you ever seen a man take a slug in the belly, Joe? You don't answer! I guess you've never seen that, huh? Skulking behind your bar like a fat bloodsucking spider. I guess you never had much chance to see any real life . . .'

'Stop it,' yelled Joe suddenly.

His voice broke. 'Stop it!' he screamed.

'Quiet,' snarled the Kid. 'You're acting like a crazy man. Quiet! – or, by Jesophat, I won't give you a chance to answer my questions, I'll plug you out of hand.'

But Joe seemed to go mad suddenly. 'I don't know anything,' he yelled. 'I don't know anything!'

With an oath, the Kid started forward a little,

his gun levelled purposefully. His eyes were full of murder. 'You can't shoot me,' yelled Joe. 'You'd have the whole saloon about your ears.'

The Kid said: 'They're making so much din back there that a single shot wouldn't be heard.'

But he grinned suddenly, wolfishly. In one swift movement he holstered his gun and sprang forward.

Joe, his mouth still open, releasing its tirade, received the first blow full in the teeth. He went over backwards, taking a chair with him, wood groaning and splintering beneath his weight.

The Kid bent, grabbed him by the front of his shirt, hauled him to his feet and slammed him upright against the wall. Cloth tore, buttons popped, Joe's flabby, sweating chest was revealed. He bared his teeth and, with the vicious desperation of a cornered rat, flung himself at the Kid.

If Joe's eyes were just plain crazy, the light that shone in the Kid's eyes now was that of unholy joy. He used his right hand only; his other dangled negligently at his side. He brought his fist around and down in a chopping blow which caught Joe on the angle of the jaw. The saloon-keeper was flung back against the wall once more. His knees began to buckle.

The Kid straightened him up again with

another blow. The back of Joe's head hit the wall with a dull thud.

'Talk, Joe!'

By way of answer Joe lashed out with his foot. Only in the nick of time did the Kid step back and even then Joe's boot grazed his shin. The Kid's lips curled back from his teeth. He moved in again. He began to use both fists now.

He beat down Joe's attempts at retaliation. Joe hit him a few times but the Kid didn't seem to feel the blows. They had no effect on him at all. Suddenly he drew back . . .

But no, Joe was not dead, although he looked an unholy mess. In fact, he was still conscious. Joe's eyes rolled pitifully, showing the whites like the bellies of dead fish . . .

Then, suddenly, Joe's eyes widened involuntarily and the Kid was warned. He flung himself down behind the desk, spinning at the same time, his gun leaping into his hand.

The room shook with gunfire.

The Kid heard the horrible sound of a bullet striking into soft flesh. He heard Joe Cater give a little animal cry. The second shot from the man in the doorway hit the light, plunging the room into darkness.

The Kid fired over the top of the desk. But he hit nothing. He realized the man had retreated into the shelter of the passage. He began to crawl swiftly on hands and knees around the desk.

He heard the thud of running feet, the blare of voices. Reinforcements were pouring into the passage.

He rose, bunched his body, dived through the window in a shower of broken glass.

He hit the ground, rolling.

CHAPTER VII

He rose slowly. He felt a little shaken and had probably collected a few bruises and cuts too. But a little experimentation soon convinced him that no bones were broken.

He was in the alley that ran alongside Joe Cater's place. There was blackness all around him but at one end of the alley he could see the faint glow of the main drag. Even as he began to move stiffly forward, half-crouching, figures blocked out that glow. He drew his gun. The boys in the saloon had thought fast.

He turned back in the other direction. There were movements back there too. He was trapped. Up till now, however, nobody seemed to have spotted him.

Back in the room he had just left, beyond the shattered window there was still blackness, silence. But his enemies could reach him that way too when they realized he wasn't waiting to blast them. He flattened himself against the wall and began to worm his way along the wall towards the back of the building, the greater blackness, the blackness from which ominous sounds already issued, sounds getting slowly, subtly louder as his enemies got nearer to him.

He was on the other side of the alley from the saloon now and, from the broken window opposite, he heard more sounds. The enemy were infiltrating into the office too.

Ages seemed to pass as he moved slowly and the sounds got louder, closing in around him. Then his groping fingers found a door. His fingers found a latch and he lifted it. He pushed the door and it opened with a faint creak. He passed through into more darkness. He closed the door gently behind him.

There was no outcry from outside. He leaned against the wall beside the door and let his muscles relax. His gun was still in his hand. The feel of it was comforting as he peered into the darkness, striving to pierce it. He listened. There was no sound. Finally, he took out a lucifer, scratched it, held the flickering flame aloft.

He seemed to be in a passage. In front of him

narrow stairs angled upwards into more stygian blackness. The match went out but he had got his bearings. He found the handrail of the stairs and began to climb.

He reached the landing and found another door. He opened it and stepped inside a room. There was a pale square of window ahead of him, the shape of a bed, white bedclothes gleaming dimly, unidentifiable shapes of furniture crouching in the darker corners.

He felt his way gingerly to the window, only to discover that it looked out on another alley. The window was partly open and from the direction of the main drag he heard those sounds again.

The hunt was on!

He found his way back to the door and, as he reached it, heard the sound of footsteps on the stairs outside. He flattened himself against the wall and, gun in hand, waited.

Light glowed beneath the door, getting steadily brighter, as if the newcomer carried a lamp. The footsteps stopped outside the door. The door opened.

In the glow, the Kid saw the huge wardrobe and dodged behind it.

Light blossomed inside the room. The door closed. The Kid, gun in hand, peeped around the edge of the wardrobe.

Right then the girl was divesting herself of her dressing-gown.

'Hold it, miss!'

With a gasp the girl turned, clutching her gown to her. She was limmed against the light and he saw that her figure was good. Her dark hair, the light behind it, was like a smoky cloud around her head.

He lowered his gun and moved around a little. She swivelled too, like an automaton, and he saw her face. Her eyes were big and dark. Her lips, open a little, gave her a startled look. But she got over her surprise quickly and her lips curled, her eyes blazed. The Kid thought she looked more beautiful than ever then.

'What are you doing here?' she stormed.

The Kid realized she wasn't a bit scared. She wasn't even embarrassed now either. She was just furious. 'The cat got your tongue?' she snapped.

The Kid grinned. He was attractive when he grinned. The hardness of his face was softened, lit up.

'I beg your pardon, miss. I guess I must've wandered into the wrong room.'

'Which one of the girls *are* you keeping company with?' she asked scathingly.

It was a relevant question but one very hard to answer. The establishment in which he stood, as now the Kid well-remembered, was a boarding-house for females. Yes, *strictly* for females. Here lived all of The Golden Calf percentage girls. In fact, all of the feminine members of Burt Hopson's organization, including The Golden Calf's top female attraction, the monumental faro-dealer known as Tombstone Kate.

The Kid had heard about the whole set-up from Grat Boyce and the boys at Diamond K. He had heard about the way the young bloods of the town had treated the set-up when it first began, the way they had tried to invade the establishment next to Cater's Place the way they would've any 'cat-house' – until Tombstone Kate sent a bunch of them scattering with buckshot in their backsides.

Evidently Burt Hopson considered that his girls should only use their charms on the menfolk at the proper time – and in the proper place: to wit, The Golden Calf.

The Kid retreated a little. He realized he still had his hat on. He took it off and made a little bow.

'It'd be more polite if you put your gun away,' the girl said.

'I'm sorry.' He holstered the gun. He retreated a little more and reached behind him for the door-knob.

'Once more I apologize for this intrusion,' he

said, 'And I'll now try to withdraw as gracefully as I can.'

The girl smiled. 'I don't believe you came up to see one of girls at all,' she said huskily. 'Not with Mother Tombstone prowling around. Not even if you got in through one of the windows. No cowboy would be that foolish.'

Her dark eyes appraised him: boldly but without rage now, or impertinence. There was no invitation in those eyes, however; they measured him as a man might have measured him, the poise of him, the look of him, the hitch of his guns. He was no ordinary cowboy and she knew it.

He forestalled her next question. 'To tell the truth I came in by the side door. It was unlocked.'

He wondered what she would do if he opened the door and went out, started down the stairs. Would she yell and give the alarm, would she let him go silently, or would she call him back?

Suddenly, through the partly-open window came a gush of sound. The mob had spilled into the alley beside the boarding-house. A bull-like voice, which the Kid did not recognize, yelled. 'He *must* be hiding someplace – he ain't had time to get away!"

The girl turned, moved lightly across to the window. She looked out, then slowly drew the curtains. She turned to face him again.

'They're looking for you. I should have guessed. Why didn't I? You're Mal Jackson. You're Pete Jackson's brother.'

'So you aim to throw me to the wolves.'

Her eyes flashed, her red lips curled. 'What do you take me for?'

'I'm sorry.' But he had to ask the inevitable question. 'What do you know about Pete Jackson?'

'I just work in this town and mind my own business. I don't know anything about Pete Jackson.' But her voice went soft as she added: 'Though he always seemed a nice sort of a fellow to me, not the sort who would bushwhack an old man who had been his friend.'

'Pete didn't bushwhack anybody.'

'And you aim to try and prove that?'

'I do.'

She gave a little sigh. 'I guess you'll have your work cut out.'

'Yes,' he said. 'I'll get out of here. Mebbe I can slip past those rats.'

'Wait!' She spun away from him and went once more to the window.

She gently moved the curtain and looked down. She came back purposefully along the side of the bed to him. 'I'm going to slip into some things and go downstairs for some chow. I'll turn out the light when I go out and you can stay here until the coast's clear. Nobody will disturb you. I'll try and let you know how things are going.'

'Miss, I wouldn't want . . .'

But she interrupted him. 'Sit on that chair over there.' She pointed. 'And turn your back.'

With a smile and a little shrug, he did as he was told. He heard her drag something a little way. It sounded like a screen. Then there was a rustle of garments and, after a moment, she said, 'You can turn round again now.'

The screen was there all right, a flimsy gaudy Japanese-type of thing. But she wasn't behind it now. She stood revealed, clad in a crisp white shirtwaist and a brown skirt, her glossy black hair pulled severely back and tied at the nape with a crisp white ribbon with a big bow. She looked like a ranch girl (with a little Spanish blood maybe) ready for her first barbecue.

But there was more than a hint of hidden fires there too . . .

Before he could rise, before he could speak, she had crossed to the door. She had her hand on the knob when she said:

'Trust me.'

It was half-question, half-statement.

He nodded. 'Thanks,' he said simply. 'And I'd like to know your name.'

'It's Josephine. Everybody calls me Jo. Jo

Lemaine. My mother was a Creole.'

'I'm mighty glad to know you, Jo.'

A smile flickered across her mouth, making dimples in her cheeks. She curtsied prettily. She said: 'Will you blow out the lamp before I open the door?'

He rose, crossed the room, blew out the lamp. As he stood in the darkness, he heard the door close behind her.

He made himself a little gap in the curtains. Then he sat on the edge of the bed in such a position that, by raising himself a little, he could see out of the window. But he didn't intend to gawp out of the window all the time, so he figured it would be safe to smoke if he made one. He found his 'makings' and rolled himself one in the darkness with practised ease. He lit up, puffed gratefully.

From outside the noise of the mob came to him in fitful gusts. But the noise gradually abated and the Kid figured that many of the hounds – probably townsfolk who had been attracted by the smell of excitement – had gotten fed up and gone back to their drinking, their gaming, their wenching.

The original hard core of the hunt remained, however. Joe Cater's friends didn't give up easily, and probably the law was taking a hand, too, by now.

The Kid wondered how that strange character Sheriff George Corletta was acting in the face of this new development. The Kid wondered if Joe Cater was dead or whether he had been able to speak, whether the boys knew who they were chasing.

And what had happened to the man who had fired the shot in the passage? Right then the Kid would have given his eye-teeth to know the identity of the man who had fired that shot.

Had Joe been plugged because he knew too much, or had he merely stopped a slug intended for the Kid? The gunmen in this territory seemed to enjoy throwing lead in the dark. And they weren't too particular about who stopped it either.

Well, other folks could play at that game. The Kid rose, dropped his cigarette on the boards and ground it carefully, with calculated savagery beneath his heel. He hitched up his gunbelt. He flexed his fingers, the long, prehensile, carefully-tended fingers of a gunfighter.

He was tired of waiting . . .

Suddenly noise bellied into the alley again. He peered through the curtain. Once more vague shapes flitted about down there. There was noise underneath him now too, in the same building. He moved soundlessly across to the door and paused there listening, thinking.

If he was spotted here Jo Lemaine might get blamed. He hadn't thought about that before. Now he cursed himself for being selfish, letting a woman cover for him. Percentage-girl or not Jo had looked too good a filly to get in Dutch through sticking her neck out for an owlhooter like him.

He eased the door open. He heard the footsteps on the stairs and closed the door again, hoping the newcomer would go on by.

But the footsteps stopped outside the door and, slowly, the door opened. The Kid drew his gun and backed slowly, making for the big wardrobe that had served him as cover once before.

In a stage whisper a voice said, 'Mr Jackson! Mal – are you there?'

'I'm here.' He moved behind her, closed the door.

He brushed against the softness of her and she hissed, 'Keep still. I can find the lamp easier than you can.'

'All right.'

He heard her pad across the room, saw the nebulous shape of her etched for a moment against the lighter square of the window. He wished he had kept a cigarette going: he was having a job to re-orient himself.

A Lucifer was scratched: flame blossomed. Next moment the Kid blinked as the yellow light hit him. He realized he still had his gun in his hand. He holstered it. But his fingers itched; a lot of noise seemed to be issuing from down below.

Jo Lemaine spoke breathlessly: 'Joe Cater's dead . . .'

'I didn't kill him. Somebody shot him from the darkness. I'm not sure whether or not the slug was meant for me . . .'

'I didn't say you did kill him. But there mustn't be any more killing. There's been too much . . . too much . . .'

'All right. I'm going now. Thank you, Miss Jo for . . .'

'Wait a minute.' Her words almost tumbled over each other. 'Some of Burt Hopson's men are downstairs talking to Tombstone. They think the man who killed Cater may be hiding here.'

'They've got a leetle mixed-up. The man who killed Joe, if I don't miss my guess, is still in the saloon. Or he might even be one of the skunks taking part in the hunt. Did they say who they were looking for?'

'I didn't hear them say that. I came up here as soon as I safely could without being missed. Those men may decide to search every room. Mother Tombstone is arguing with them. But Burt Hopson is her boss too, so she'll have to give way eventually. All the activity seems to be centred out front now, so if you move fast I think you'll be able to slip out the back way.'

There was a question he had wanted to ask ever since he had met her. Before he left her, although he knew he was wasting time, he felt he must ask it. But he made it oblique.

'I can't understand why a girl like you works for Burt Hopson.'

Her face froze up. He cursed himself. Her reply was oblique too. 'I don't work for Hopson the way many other people work for him. I seldom see the man. I dance a little, I circulate among the customers, I do my job. I'm an orphan.' She smiled but with no mirth. 'Even an orphan must work.'

'A beautiful girl like you should be married.'

'Who'd marry a percentage-girl?'

'For Pete's sake! You're no ordinary percentage girl. I've only known you a half-hour or so but I can tell that . . .'

She ended the conversation with a brief chopping movement of her hand. 'You're wasting time, Mr Jackson. Please go.'

'The name is Mal, Jo. You've used it once – you can use it again.'

'All right, Mal. Go!'

'I'm going.' But, his hand at the door, he paused again. 'Thank you, Jo. And if ever I can do anything to repay you, please let me know.'

'I have done nothing, Mal,' she said. Her voice softened. 'Go with God.'

He echoed the ancient Spanish farewell, adding, '*Adios, chiquita.*' Then he opened the door and stepped out into the passage and heard the sound of bootheels upon the stairs.

He moved back into the shadows. There was only one man and he was staring glassily straight in front of him. The Kid could have touched him. It was Sheriff George Corletta. He opened Joe's door without knocking and went inside. The door closed behind him.

The Kid waited. There was no sound of raised voices from inside the room. But now, from down below, clamour rose. The Kid went down the stairs.

At the side door he paused. He looked back up the stairs. There was no movement up there, no sound. But the sounds still came from outside and from the front of the building. To the right of him was another door which presumably led to the front of the place. The Kid expected this door to fly open at any moment.

He eased the side door open gently. The alley seemed to be quiet. He opened the door wider. Then the thing he had feared, happened. The other door was opened and a bulky shape came through. A huge woman with bright red hair. The

Kid had never met Tombstone Kate, but he figured this apparition couldn't be anything else but that fabulous lady.

She was half-turned away from him, calling to somebody behind her. He didn't know whether she spotted him or not. He slipped through the door and closed it gently behind him.

He paused for a split second, his hand on his gun. Then he spun on his heels and ran down the alley towards the back of the building.

His riding-boots with their scuffed high heels had not been made for running. He lurched and stumbled. He was savage with himself because he had to run. There were no sounds yet of immediate pursuit. He turned the corner and charged full tilt into a man coming in the opposite direction.

The man staggered. Steel glinted in the darkness. The muzzle of a gun was in perilous proximity to the Kid's stomach. He brought up his foot, heel tilted. He felt the sharp heel grind against the bone of the man's knee. The man cried out with sudden agony. The gun wavered. The Kid drove both fists savagely forward, beating them into the man's face. The man went down, jerked a little then lay still.

The Kid ran on.

He reached his horse. Nobody, it seemed, had spotted the trusty beast. He mounted. He was not challenged from the darkness. But not until he was out of town did he set the beast at a gallop in the direction of Diamond K.

There was no hue and cry. Nevertheless, after he had been riding some time and had set the horse's pace to a steady lope, he thought he heard signs of pursuit.

He halted, listening. The drumming of hoofs was like the sound of Indian drums in the distant night.

The riders were coming hard and they were coming fast.

Ahead of the Kid was a jumbled, fantastically-shaped rock outcrop. The man urged his horse behind this and waited.

As the riders got nearer they seemed to slacken their pace. Then the Kid heard them talking. He couldn't make out the words but suddenly his ears pinpointed one particular voice. Lilting, Southern; molasses and cream.

There was no mistaking it! It was the voice of the coloured ranny, Mortimer Jaques.

The sounds faded into the distance.

CHAPTER VIII

The figure came out into the blaze of light from the open bunkhouse door. The light glinted on the barrel of a shotgun.

The Kid's hand dropped to his Colt. But Grat Boyce recognized him and lowered the shotgun.

'F'r Pete's sake, Mal, where've you bin? We thought you'd get back here before we did.' Grat led the way back into the bunkhouse. The rest of the boys waited there.

Grat turned again. 'You're the coyote who caused the ruckus in town, no doubt.'

'Yes, I guess so,' said the Kid cautiously.

'An' plugged Joe Cater,' put in another man.

'No,' said the Kid, and waited.

A diversion was caused by the cook appearing with hot coffee and eats. The Kid joined the others at the table and set to. Presently, through a mouthful of hotcakes, Grat Boyce said:

'The Brannigans figured you'd make for town an' try to persuade somebody to talk. Betty Lou was scared for you, venturing back into that den o' wolves on your lonesome – she rode here an' told us. So a few of us went to town, too. We were there when the shooting started. But, for a bit, nobody seemed to know what it was all about.'

'I didn't kill Joe Cater,' said the Kid. 'Who did?'

'Nobody seemed to know. You were the most likely suspect, however, though nobody had seen you, nobody knew you were in town even. We pretended to join in the mob. Then, after a while, when nobody was caught, we figured that, if you had been in town you would've lit out for the ranch by now.'

'I had lit out,' said the Kid. 'I heard you behind me and, thinking you were a posse, pulled off to the side of the trail until you had gone by. As a matter of fact I recognized Morty's voice but I didn't know whether he had maybe gotten mixed up with a bunch from town or not, so I didn't holler.'

'Yeh, you're liable to run across Morty in all kinds of strange company,' said Grat Boyce.

The coloured ranny grinned and said, 'Shore thing!'

The Kid went on to tell of how Joe Cater had been shot. And he learned it was as much of a mystery to these boys as it was to him.

Time was taken out to really concentrate on the eats; everybody doing so. The Kid was thoughtful. He thought about Betty Lou. There was a peach of a girl for you!

But he was a little peeved about her riding to the Diamond K on his behalf. At the moment the night-range was lousy with hardcases, some of whom – despite high-fangled Eastern ideas about Western chivalry – would not hesitate to molest a lone woman. He hoped Betty Lou had got back all right. He voiced his anxiety to Grat Boyce who assured him that two of the men had escorted Betty Lou back home safely.

'Some girl!' opinioned Grat Boyce. There was no flippancy in his voice, just great respect.

'D'you think the sheriff and his mob will go to the Brannigans' spread looking for me again?' asked the Kid.

Grat Boyce said, 'If they do they'll get a hot reception from Ma an' Curly an' the boys. There's no reason why they should go there though. After all, they didn't find you there the last time they called an' they'd have no reason to believe they'd find you there now. They might even make a *pasear* in this direction instead.'

The Kid grinned wolfishly. 'That'll be just dandy.'

But he was grave again the next moment, thinking. He seemed to be doing an unconscionable amount of thinking lately. Not that he wasn't having plenty of action too, though: enough of that to fill any man's belly. He had come back to Pendant in the first place for peace, and time to think. He had seen no peace at all. He hadn't had time to think but the thoughts had come all the same, though a little jumbled.

Women made a man think. And his thoughts switched now from Betty Lou Brannigan to the other beautiful filly he had gotten tangled with since he hit Pendant, Jo Lemaine. Two girls from two widely different walks of Western life, yet two girls who in their fire and independence, were very much alike.

... Or was he maybe seeing Jo, because she had saved his bacon tonight, through rose-coloured spectacles? He could not forget how Sheriff Corletta had entered Jo's room without knocking. Jo had not given any alarm. But if there was an understanding between her and the sheriff – the kind of understanding you would expect when a man entered a female's room without knocking – maybe she had spilled the beans by now!

Grat Boyce was posting guards, sending out others to relieve night-riders, urging others to get some shut-eye. He told the Kid there was nothing much he could do about anything right now, except wait. He needed sleep too. The Kid saw the wisdom of this and headed for his bunk. Pretty soon he was sunk in a healthy, dreamless slumber.

He was in the corral with Grat Boyce and two more men early the following morning when they saw the three riders approaching them across the sunwashed range. Presently they recognized Ma Brannigan and Lawyer Kramer, the latter seated with hunched awkwardness on his horse. But the third man, tall, black-haired, dude-looking, was a stranger to them.

Ma, without preliminaries, sang out, 'Like to see you in private, Mal.'

Grat Boyce looked curious. But he said: 'Use the bunkhouse. There's nobody there.'

Once inside the bunkhouse Ma introduced the dude-looking stranger as Henry Crocott, a lawyer from back East. Grocott's grip was strong. Despite his fancy clothes and pink well-barbered look he seemed, on closer inspection, a straight man and a powerful one.

Lawyer Kramer had kept his promise and acquired a slick Eastern lawyer to give a decision on the Luke Price inheritance case. Lawyer Kramer, despite his weasel-like and unprepossessing manner was as straight as any two-bit Western lawyer could hope to be. He preened him now as the powerful Henry Grocott gave his pronouncement in a cultured, well-modulated courtroom voice.

This very interesting case which had been brought to Grocott's notice was unique even in *his* experience. But he was pleased to say it was not unique in the annals of law and, by study and consultation with other lawyers, he had finally arrived at a conclusion.

The Kid was of the opinion that Mr Grocott talked too much. Still, he was an Easterner, and a lawyer to boot, so maybe there was some excuse for him. The man had his wits about him anyway. The little runt, Kramer, fawned on him as if he was royalty or somep'n. They waited patiently as Grocott's sonorous voice rolled on.

But the lawyer, now he was actually down to cases, didn't waste any more words.

Widowed, childless Luke Price had left his holdings, everything he had to his foreman, Peter Jackson. Peter was dead so everything went now to Peter's wife, Lucy. (Grocott even had all his names right.)

Peter was alleged to have murdered his employer and benefactor but Peter had been killed himself before this had been proved. A man was innocent until proven guilty . . .

'So here's what I advise,' said Grocott. 'Mrs Jackson can move to this ranch and take it over. If Peter Jackson did not kill his employer, soon perhaps the real killer will be unmasked. Mrs Jackson will stay here and we will wait . . .'

The door from the kitchen opened and Grat Boyce stuck his head out. He said: 'The cook's fixing you folks some coffee. It'll be out any minute now.'

Henry Grocott bowed slightly. 'Thank you, my friend.'

He sat down. Everybody else followed suit. Evidently, for the moment, he had said all he meant to say.

He took a deep breath, expanding his barrel-like chest. 'I like this territory. It's *big*. I've a mind to settle out here someday.'

After a time Grocott rode away with Ma Brannigan and Lawyer Kramer. Grocott said he aimed to stay a while and get in some riding and to Hades with business back East for a while. Before they left, the Kid took Ma aside and told her that as soon as darkness fell he'd pay a visit to the Brannigan spread to see Betty Lou and Lucy and the kids. Ma didn't argue with him.

The day passed slowly as the Kid mooched irritably around the ranch. There were no visitors. No more news came in from town. Diamond K riders, moseying in from time to time, reported that things were quiet on the range too, no sign of prowlers and watchers.

Things were too quiet for the Kid's liking. He had a feeling it was just the quiet before a big blow.

But at last night fell and he saddled up and made tracks for the Brannigan spread. It was quiet there, too. They hadn't had any vistors.

Lawyer Kramer had left pretty early on business but Henry Grocott had stayed to talk to Lucy. He had only just gone. Ma asked him to stay the night but he said he'd already gotten fixed up in town. Besides, he wanted to look the place over.

'He's the soul of good manners,' said Ma, who hadn't seemed to notice such things before. 'An' when he gets off law he's quite human. Despite myself, I kinda took a shine to the man.'

'Yeh,' said the Kid non-committally.

Betty Lou came in then with the chow, her eyes shining like stars as she exchanged glances with him. The kids were romping and their Uncle Mal joined in, but found himself suddenly shy of Arrabella: she had grown into such a big gel. He was preoccupied, too, with something else Ma had told him.

Lucy had refused to go to the Diamond K until everything was finally decided.

'Possession is nine points of the law,' the Kid had said. He was getting quite slick at this legal jargon. But Ma told him that Henry Grocott had already used that argument – and more cleverly, too. But without success.

Supper was served and everybody set to. But things were interrupted by the sudden appearance of the foreman, Curly Randle.

He said a woman on horseback had called at the ranch looking for Mal Jackson. She wouldn't come up but was waiting out by the corral.

The Kid stood up. All eyes were upon him. He avoided Betty Lou's eyes, the puzzled, hurt look in them. He said:

'How did she know she'd find me here?'

'She didn't,' said Curly. 'She says she just came on the off-chance. She's got a message for you.'

The Kid didn't ask who the girl was. He figured it couldn't be anybody else but Jo Lemaine. The message must be important.

'I'll go see,' he said and left hurriedly with Curly.

But the woman at the corral was not Jo. It was another dance-hall girl of about Jo's age. She introduced herself as Kate Prather, Jo's best friend. She said Jo was in trouble.

Kate had been riding hard. She was obviously worried and distressed.

'Take it easy, honey,' said the Kid. 'Come inside an' rest an' have a cup of coffee.'

'No. I haven't got time.' Kate was vehement. 'You must help, Mr Jackson. You must come back with me and see what you can do.'

The Kid turned, spoke to Curly. The foreman went to fetch the Kid's horse.

'While we're waiting you better tell me what it's all about.'

So the girl told him.

Burt Hopson had found out that Jo Lemaine hid Mal after the Joe Cater killing. A couple of Hopson's men – with Sheriff Corletta in the uneasy offing – had taken Jo away. Jo had managed to get a message to her friend, Kate: 'Tell Mal Jackson'. The Hopson boys were rough boys: Kate was scared what might happen to Jo.

Curly had returned with the Kid's horse. The Kid was glad he hadn't taken off his gun back there in the house. He gave Curly a hurried message for the ladies. Then he mounted, joined Kate again.

'Let's go.'

They didn't slow down until they could see the lights of Pendant. Then Kate, after getting her breath back, was able to answer a few more questions.

Burt Hopson's quarters were in back of The Golden Calf. Some of his men had rooms back there too. Now that Hopson had shown his hand, he probably would not hesitate to keep Jo somewhere at The Golden Calf for questioning.

They approached the place from the back. This, in contrast to the naphtha-flared brilliance of the front of the place, was dark and gloomy, though sounds of revelry came on the wind.

This was man's work so, after thanking Kate, the Kid made her go back to her lodgings. Luckily, she was not on duty that night so wouldn't have been missed.

The Kid tethered his horse by a rickety fence, the remains of a burnt cabin, its ashes still rustling in the wind. He eased his gun in its holster and approached the back door of The Golden Calf.

If danger lurked he had expected it to blossom from the door or windows rather than anywhere else. Consequently, he was taken completely by surprise when a man stepped from the blackness beside him and said, 'Put up your hands.'

The man was just a dark bulk. A gun-barrel gleamed, levelled steadily. The voice had been deep, resonant. Something familiar about it. But it sounded like it meant business. So, letting go the thought of a quick draw, the Kid raised his hands.

'Turn to your right an' start walking,' said the voice. A little puzzled, the Kid did as he was told. They moved away from The Golden Calf to the building next door then stopped again.

'Go through the door and climb the stairs,' said the voice. 'And remember I'm right behind you.'

Then, opening the door, the Kid remembered what building stood next door to The Golden Calf. It was Lawyer Kramer's office. Then, as he climbed the stairs, he guessed the identity of the man with the gun and he was even more puzzled.

A thread of light shone beneath the door at the top of the stairs. The Kid opened the door and went in. It was the back door of Lawyer Kramer's office and now the runty lawyer sat behind his desk and blinked at the newcomer.

The Kid turned slowly, to face Henry Grocott.

The latter had the bigger surprise. 'Jackson,' he exclaimed. 'What are you doing here?'

The Kid said: 'I don't aim to talk while you've got a gun pointed at my belly.'

But Lawyer Kramer gave the answer to Grocott's question. In his dry precise voice he said:

'Perhaps Mr Jackson is here in the capacity of a knight-errant, too,'

'Do you know Miss Jo Lemaine?' asked Grocott, lowering the gun.

But the Kid was still cautious. 'Yes, I know her.'

'Did you know that a snake called Burt Hopson was keeping her captive next door?'

'Yes, I did, that's why I came. But how did you come to know this. You're a stranger in town. What's Jo Lemaine to you?'

'It's a long story, friend,' said Grocott. There was a subtle new note in his voice. ' 'Tis my regret, I haven't seen Jo for some years. But I hope to see her again as soon as possible,' he jerked the gun, 'and I'm taking this along to make certain I do so.'

'You're no ordinary Eastern slicker.'

'You're right there, amigo.' Grocott's grin gave a boyish look to his heavily handsome face. 'I was raised in New Mexico. I went back East to seek my fame and fortune. I found it all right but I'm beginning to feel that I missed it in some ways too. The last few days have made a new man of me and to see Jo Lemaine again will be the culmination of a great time.' He paused.

'But we're wasting time!' he added.

His floridity still got in the Kid's craw somewhat. 'How did you know Burt Hopson had Miss Jo?' he asked.

Grocott stabbed with a big hand. 'My associate there. I guess nothing much goes on in this town that he doesn't know about.'

The Kid turned and looked at Lawyer Kramer.

The latter smiled. He looked almost human. His stock went up quite some in the Kid's estimation. 'Are you with me, Mal?'

'I'm with you, Henry.'

'Me, too,' said Lawyer Kramer. The words were boyish. And compared with the wizened little man's usual tone of voice, the manner of speaking them was boyish too.

The two men, on their way to the door, halted in their tracks. They turned on him in surprise, wondering if he was making some grim joke, though he wasn't a joking type of man.

But he had risen and was rummaging in a drawer of his desk. He came up with a formidable looking Frontier-model Colt in his scrawny fist.

'This is hardly ethical, Hiram,' said Henry Grocott, in deep half-bantering tones.

'I'm sixty years of age,' said Hiram Kramer. 'I guess it's time I became a little un-ethical.'

Despite his implacable purpose, the Kid grinned. The little lawyer was turning up trumps after all.

The Kid said: 'Can you handle that thing?'

'I don't keep it for a paperweight,' retorted Hiram Kramer, with some of his old waspishness. He opened his coat, methodically undid the bottom two buttons of his vest and tucked the gun into the waistband of his trousers.

The two other men exchanged glances. 'Let's go,' said Henry Grocott.

They went.

All three of them.

They were all out in the darkness and the door shut behind them when the neighbouring door, the back door to The Golden Calf, opened suddenly, letting out a gush of light.

The three men flattened themselves against the clapboard walls and watched and listened. A shadow was thrown across the yellow path of light but nobody had appeared yet. There was a murmur of voices but no words could be distinguished, or even the tone of the voices; the sound was just a guttural mumble.

Suddenly the light went out. Then a figure appeared, a vague shape in the darkness; ran across the sod and disappeared. The Kid was starting forward when Grocott laid a restraining hand on his arm. 'I think the man inside the door is still watching.'

The Kid realized the older man was probably right. Hoofbeats sounded, faded away in the distance. Then there was the sound of the door being softly closed. The three men moved again. The Kid was a guerrilla fighter by nature, no stranger to this kind of nocturnal winding. But Grocott – and even little Kramer bringing up the rear – might have been his maraudering pardners for years, judging by the way they acted.

They reached the corner of the other building. The place was all in darkness again. The windows were tightly shuttered. 'I guess we might as well use the door,' said the Kid. 'If it's unlocked.'

The words froze on his lips as footsteps sounded on the dirt of the alley. Once more the three men flattened themselves against the wall, hid themselves in the blackness there.

The man passed so close to them that any one of them could have reached out and touched him. The darkness through which he walked was not as deep as the darkness in which they crouched. They should have seen the white blob of his face the way they had seen the white indistinguishable blob of the other man's face. But this time there was no white blob and, as the Kid watched the man's very distinctive half loping he realized why. He had no doubt. No other man he knew walked that way. The man's face did not show in the darkness because the man's face was black. The man was Morty Jaques.

The Kid almost challenged the coloured ranny. But a sudden spasm of caution prevented him.

Morty had his horse stashed out there in the darkness too, and pretty soon they heard him riding away. 'Lot of traffic around here tonight,' hissed Henry Grocott.

The other two did not speak. The Kid did not disclose that he knew the identity of the second man. He wondered if Hiram Kramer had recognized Morty too.

They went on to the door, only to find it locked, and very stout and immovable to boot.

'I guess we better try a window after all,' said the Kid and proceeded to do so.

The stout blade of his jack-knife did the trick. He lifted the heavy sash and, one by one, they climbed from their familiar darkness into the greater darkness inside. The Kid closed the window after them.

It was darkness like a black velvet blanket and there was no sound in it either. It was as if everybody in The Golden Calf had heard them enter and was waiting in breathless ominous silence for their next move.

The other two men started when Kramer said in a soft voice:

'I've been in here before. This is Burt Hopson's fancy soundproof study.'

'I guess he'd hardly keep the girl in here then,' said Grocott.

'I did some legal business for Hopson when this place was being built,' said Kramer. 'I saw the plans. There is a big cellar where the better class liquor and wine is stored. It is, in fact, the only cellar in Pendant.'

'Do you think you can lead us to it?'

'I think so.'

They found their way to the door, only to find it was locked and there was no key.

The Kid took out his gun and, with a single shot, blew the lock apart.

CHAPTER IX

When the reverberations of the shot had died away, Hiram Kramer said sternly, 'That was a rather foolish thing to do.'

'You said the room was soundproof didn't you?' retorted the Kid.

He swung the door open and stepped into the passage. Their guns ready in their fists the other two followed him. A hanging hurricane lantern glowed ahead of thom. Sounds of revelry came to them.

'I had better lead the way,' said Hiram Kramer, and brushed past the Kid.

The latter admired the little man's guts. But evidently the shot had not been heard, for they reached the cellar-head without mishap.

This door opened, revealing a flight of stone steps, which they descended. At the bottom was another door, very stout, studded with brass. This was locked and there was no key in the lock.

The three men grouped themselves in the little lobby by the door. The Kid rapped on the door with the butt of his gun.

'Jo,' he called, keeping his voice as low as possible. 'Jo, this is Mal Jackson, can you hear me?'

There was a reply. Muffled, but audible. A glad voice. 'Mal! Yes! Yes, I hear you.'

The Kid turned, his keen eyes regarded Lawyer Kramer. 'Looks like I'll have to blow this lock apart too. Will you go an' shut the top door and stay there an' give us warning if you hear any commotion. I take it that this part of the building *isn't* soundproof.'

'I don't imagine so,' said Kramer with a thin little smile. But he went docilely back to the stairs. Evidently he realized that at this kind of nefarious violence the lithe boy with the chilling eyes was his master.

Kramer reached the top of the steps and looked out. He gave the all-clear sign before closing the door and, gun in hand, crouching against it.

The Kid called, 'Jo! Listen!'

'I'm listening, Mal.'

'I'll have to shoot the door open. Get out of the line of fire.'

After a moment she called, 'All right. You can

start shooting now.'

The Kid stood back a little, levelled his gun and fired. But it took another shot before the heavy door swung open.

The cellar was brilliantly lit and from among the rows and rows of barrels, the girl came forward to meet them. She was a little dishevelled but, at first sight, seemed to be unharmed.

'Mal . . .'

Then she stopped. Henry Grocott had come past the Kid, had come right into the light, so that she could see him clearly.

'Hallo, Jo,' he said softly.

Her eyes left Mal then, and came to rest fully on the big lawyer.

'Harry! Harry Grocott!' There was a soft lilt in her voice. There was, suddenly, a new light in her dark eyes too.

The Kid had seen that light in a woman's eyes before: he saw it in the eyes of Betty Lou when she looked at him And now the two other people came together, took each other's hands as if he wasn't there any more.

The Kid whirled at a clatter of feet on the steps.

'What's keeping you?' called Hiram Kramer in a stage whisper.

'Let's go,' said the Kid peremptorily and, like automatons, the man and the girl followed him.

In the passage they ran into a white-aproned barman. Before he could open his mouth the Kid slugged him.

'He recognized us,' said Lawyer Kramer.

'I ought to slit his throat.' said the Kid savagely. He sounded as if all that he needed was a word from one of his companions. But one didn't come and he grinned wolfishly and led them on.

'I vote we all go back to the Diamond K,' he said. 'Then if that mob gets after us we'll be ready for them, and have some strength to help us.'

Jo said she felt fit enough to ride. Grocott already had a horse ready for her. They hit the trail.

Strangely enough, they reached the Diamond K without hearing any sounds of pursuit. There was no woman at the ranch, so the cook took over. During Pendant's embryo range-war the fat flapjack merchant had proved himself a rough but competent medico. However, Jo Lemaine assured him that, though a little dishevelled, she was quite unhurt.

She explained that up to the time of her rescue Burt Hopson and his roughs had only bombarded her with questions. Before they left her for the last time Hopson had said that if she didn't talk at the next visit, he was going to lock her in the cellar with three of his roughs, who as he put it cynically 'had a way with women', and leave her to their tender mercies.

As Jo got to this point of her narrative the Diamond K boys forthwith wanted to ride and take The Golden Calf apart.

'Yeh,' said the Kid. 'That'll have to come – soon.'

But Jo had not quite finished her tale. She had to explain just why Burt Hopson had her picked up: and the Kid was much concerned with this.

It seemed that when he had left Jo's room Sheriff George Corletta had spotted him in the darkness of the hallway but had pretended not to.

'I'm not sure why he did this,' said Jo. 'Maybe he was scared to show his hand in case you killed him . . .'

She paused, looking at the Kid. The latter did not speak but his lips curled as he thought of the sheriff, his pale blue eyes were like chips of fiery ice.

Jo went on: 'I probably know as much about George Corletta as anybody else – and perhaps more than most. I know that he was drummed out of the Rangers for cowardice . . .'

A buzz of comments and exclamations greeted this pronouncement. 'Can you beat that?' said one voice. 'An' him a lawman!'

'George Corletta is nothing to me,' said Jo, and this time she was looking straight at Henry

Grocott. 'Though, until last night, I thought he was. We were friendly. I guess that, in some way, I was sorry for him. Women are funny creatures. I guess I thought he had had a kind of raw deal from life. Sometimes when I feel low I'm liable to think I've had a raw deal myself . . .'

Jo paused again. For the last few sentences it had been almost as if she was talking to herself. Or maybe she was just talking to Henry Grocott. Utterly disregarding the rest of the bunch – tough cowhands to whom any show of sentiment was anathema – Henry had gotten hold of her hand. Now she gave a little spurt of laughter. Then just as suddenly was grave again; and her voice went on:

'That night George barged into my room without knocking and wanted to know what Mal Jackson had been doing there. I sent him back out with a flea in his ear and like a cur he went yelping to his boss, Burt Hopson. Hopson sent two of his roughs for me but I managed to give my friend Kate a message for Mal. Hopson thought I was in league with Mal and the 'ranching element', as he called it, that was against him.'

She finished, took the steaming cup of coffee the cook had brought her, and sipped it gratefully.

'Well,' said the Kid, 'it seems that Hopson has shown his hand completely this time. The fight's in the open. We've got to fight fire by fire.'

Everybody was agreed on this. Even the cautious Hiram Kramer did not raise any objection.

'Will they attack here tonight do you think?' asked one man.

The Kid rose. 'God, if that barman I slugged recognized me and gave the alarm they might think we were taking Jo to Ma Brannigan's.'

But Grat Boyce put his oar in now. 'It's no good jumping to conclusions and a bunch of us riding there an' leaving this place unprotected. I'll send a couple of the boys to reconnoitre. While they're about it they can warn Ma an' Curly an' his boys.'

'Yeh,' agreed the Kid. 'And we oughta find some way the two ranches can signal to each other.'

'Both ranch houses have rises nearby,' put in Mortimer Jaques, the coloured ranny. 'It wouldn't take long to build a bonfire on each of them, plenty of grease-soaked stuff that'd flare up quickly.'

'A good idea,' said Grat Boyce.

The Kid said nothing. But he was looking at Morty Jaques. He remembered suddenly where he had last seen Morty and a question trembled on his lips. But he choked it: maybe now was not quite the right time to voice it. He made a resolve that he would keep an eye on Morty however. The coloured boy did not seem to see anything strange in the Kid's demeanour. He grinned, seemingly proud of his signal-fire suggestion.

Grat Boyce sent a couple of men out, detailed others to build a fire. The Kid was glad that Morty wasn't one of the men under orders: the young trouble-shooter didn't want the coloured man to get out of his sight.

The Kid suggested that Jo might be better off at Ma Brannigan's place. But the girl, exchanging glances with Henry Grocott, elected to stay where she was. The cook put clean blankets on an empty bunk and, fully-clothed except for her shoes, she lay down to rest.

Revolvers, rifles and shotguns were checked and cleaned as the men got ready for their vigil. Maybe nothing would happen; but, as one man, they hoped it would. And, if it didn't, they were quite prepared to do the attacking themselves, carrying the fight into the enemy camp. After hearing Jo Lemaine's story their blood was afire and they were raring to go.

Jo Lemaine fell asleep and Henry Grocott started to tell Hiram Kramer and the Kid of how he had first met the girl.

He divulged the fact – a fact already known, it seemed, to his old friend, Hiram – that before he became a successful Eastern slicker he once had a little practice in the border hell-hole of San Antone.

Into this office one day wandered a disconsolate young girl. She had been playing a piano at a nearby dancehall and had had the sack because the proprietor affirmed she wasn't fancy enough for the customers. Henry Grocott, however, thought she was one of the most beautiful girls he had ever seen. The dance-hall proprietor still owed her some wages and refused to pay. She wanted Henry to get the money for her.

He got it all right. And collected a badly-bruised pair of knuckles for interest. He nominated Jo Lemaine for a teacher's post that was vacant in the small local school. They became firm friends. There was talk among the biddies of San Antone that they were betrothed.

'I had to go East for a conference,' said Henry. 'I didn't have time to tell Jo of my plans. I was away much longer than I expected – two weeks in fact. When I got back Jo had gone. Nobody knew where she had gone. Maybe she thought I had run out on her. But I hadn't. I came back for her. I wanted to marry her, take her back East with me. I've made plenty of trips West since then, looking for her. I never found her.'

Henry's voice faded away, then burst out again angrily. 'When tonight, Hiram told me about the girl Hopson had imprisoned and who that girl was, I wanted to go in an' tear the Golden Calf to pieces.' He looked ruefully at his wizened colleague. 'Hiram talked me out of it. For the best too, I guess – everything turned out all right . . .'

The two men came back from the Brannigan place. They had ridden hard. They said Curly and the boys were getting ready. A signal-fire was being built too, they would light it if the Pendant mob attacked. Curly sent word that the Diamond K must do the same if they were attacked first.

Jo Lemaine still slept peacefully. Morty Jaques got up and, with that smooth silence that characterized all his movements, left the bunkhouse. Probably the Kid was the only person who saw him go. The Kid got up and, just as silently, followed him.

Standing in the shadow of an old tree he watched Morty lead his horse from the stables and mount up, setting the beast at a walking pace. The Kid waited till the darkness had swallowed the rider up before he got his own horse out and followed. Those of the Diamond K boys who weren't in the bunkhouse were still building the bonfire on the little rise behind the ranch. The Kid did not think anybody had seen Morty and him leave.

Out of sight of the ranch now, he heard the thud

of hoofs up ahead. The coloured ranny had set his horse to a gallop. The Kid urged his own mount to greater speed. After a time he realized he was on the trail to town; Morty was evidently making for Pendant.

The Kid reined in his mount at intervals to listen. At about the fourth time he realized that now there was no sound of drumming hoofs above the gentle soughing of the night-winds. If he turned the bend in the trail he would be upon the clump of cottonwoods which lay beside the trail midway between Pendant and the Diamond K. Had Morty heard his pursuer? Was he lying in wait there in the cottonwoods?

The Kid dismounted, tethered his horse to a clump of mesquite that was conveniently near. He continued on foot, his boots making no sound on the stunted grass. The cottonwoods came in sight. He went nearer, half-crouching now, his hand on his gun.

He saw the horse tethered nearby. Then he heard the voices. They did not cease and he knew he had not been spotted. He could not distinguish any words. He reached a tree on the outskirts of the ring and crouched behind it as he saw the two dim figures in the tiny clearing ahead of him.

One of them was Morty Jaques, the other a woman; and now the Kid heard the woman's voice.

'Please take care, honey.'

It was a Southern voice, a soft, caressing burnt-round-the-edges voice rather like Morty's own, though not so deep.

The Kid knew that there were coloured dance-hall girls in town, well-favoured high-yellows that were worthy of any man's regard. He was surprised, even a little chagrined. Had Morty merely rode out here to keep a rendezvous with a coffee and cream filly?

Morty said: 'I'll be careful. I've got to get back now.'

The two figures mingled, then broke apart again. The Kid let himself sink flat into the grass. But Morty and the girl went in the other direction and the Kid figured the girl probably had a horse out of sight and her boyfriend was walking her to it.

The Kid rose and ran back to his own horse and led the beast well off the trail. A few moments later he heard the other two horses moving; one away from him, the other in his direction.

But Morty sped by on the trail and after a few moments the Kid followed him.

He stopped from time to time to listen. Seemed like Morty was speeding right back to the ranch.

The Kid had covered about half the distance

when he heard the shot from up ahead.

Once more he reined in his horse and listened. Now there was no sound of hoofbeats from up ahead, only the dirge-like soughing of the wind

The Kid took his rifle from its scabbard and placed it on the saddle in front of him. He set his horse at a walking pace, straining his eyes and ears all the time.

Had Morty been bushwhacked? And, if so, why? And how? Then the Kid remembered the small outcrop of rocks just off the trail ahead of him. Like the clump of cottonwoods he had recently left, it was a minor landmark. A man could lie behind those rocks and draw a bead on a man on the trail. Even in the darkness a bushwhacker would be near enough to get a decent shot . . .

The Kid was surprised when he heard the hoofbeats start up again. After a while he set his horse at a faster pace too.

He reached the outcrop of rocks. Nothing happened. He reined in and dismounted. He went over to the rocks. He listened a while before scratching a Lucifer, cupping the flame in his hands. Something gleamed among the rocks. He bent and picked it up. It was a brass shellcase. He pocketed it. He went back to his horse and remounted.

When the Kid entered the bunkhouse Morty

was sitting with the rest of the boys. Nobody commented on the Kid's absence. Jo Lemaine was still sleeping. Henry Grocott sat near her, looking at her. Hiram Kramer sat nearby reading a tattered news-sheet. At the big central table a poker-school was under way.

CHAPTER X

Grat Boyce came in from the back and broke the card-school up. He gave orders to some of the men. He wanted them to clear the forecourt and the yard of the ranch, so that if the Pendant mob attacked they'd have little cover in their approach.

A bunch of men followed Grat out. After a moment Morty Jaques went too. The Kid followed him. The Kid paused outside, closing the door behind him. He watched.

Men seemed to be moving in all directions. Some had discovered lumber that needed burning and were carrying it around to the fire. Others were moving wheelbarrows, barrels, buckets and other miscellaneous items that tend to accumulate in the vicinity of a ranch house. Much of this stuff could have been used for cover.

The Kid saw Grat Boyce carrying a huge

wooden box towards the barn. Grat was alone, there was nobody near him But now Morty came into view – he seemed to be hugging shadows – and followed Grat.

The ramrod didn't seem to be aware of his shadower, and disappeared in the barn. Morty kept right on after him. The Kid, taking advantage of the blacker shadows too, followed Morty. Light shone dimly from the barn.

He reached the open doors of the barn and stiffened to the wall against them and was just in time to hear Morty's first words as the coloured man confronted Grat Boyce.

'The game's up, Grat.'

The reply came, surprised, a little querulous. 'Morty! What's eating you? You sound mad about something.'

'You'd be mad if you'd been shot by a filthy bushwhacker. You almost took my ear off with that slug from your rifle. You ought to've made sure, Grat. I know too much, you've suspected that, you ought to've made sure, Grat, you ought-to've shut mah mouth for good.'

'My rifle . . . Morty, what in tarnation are you babbling about?' Grat laughed harshly, without amusement.

'Quit foxing,' said Morty. 'I've been watching you for days. I followed you to town earlier tonight. I saw you in back of The Golden Calf. I saw Burt Hopson let you out again. You've allus coveted this ranch. You're working hand in glove with Hopson to try an' get it.' Morty's molasses and cream tones rose suddenly, became full of menace.

'You're a stinking, four-flushing snake an' I'm callin' you out.'

The Kid moved again but, even as he did, the shooting started.

The sound of it reverberated in the enclosed space of the barn; slugs whined and ricocheted wickedly; a horse screamed in terror and pain.

The Kid ran through the doors, half-crouching, gun in hand. The clamour died. The barn was in darkness now, for somebody had shot the lamp out. The Kid heard a man gasping with pain; he heard running footsteps; 'Morty,' he called softly.

'Here – Mal – here.'

He almost fell over the form on the ground. 'Morty. How . . .?'

'Just my side. God, he's fast! I ought to've shot him down like a dog. I'll be all right. Watch him, Mal . . . watch him . . . Go on. Git! I'm all right, I tell yuh.'

The Kid found Morty's hand, pressed it, rose, went on.

The barn had a small back door, which now was

swinging open. The Kid dived through the aperture, head low. A slug almost parted his hair. He hit the ground, twisted against the wall, came right side up. Another slug slammed into the door jamb. A sliver of wood jabbed knife-like into the Kid's cheek. He fired at flashes in the darkness in front of him, then dived for more cover. He reached the corner of the ranch house and crouched against it.

There was a lull in the shooting and he heard running feet. Men were coming round the side of the barn. It was quicker than rushing right through the barn – and maybe they figured it was less dangerous too.

A figure flitted away there in the darkness. The Kid took a potshot at it and missed. Then Grat reached the shelter of a boulder, one of the articles of cover which the boys hadn't been able to move.

Slugs sought the Kid out, a veritable screaming barrage of them. It sounded as if Grat was fanning the hammer of his gun. The corner of the ranch house gave very little cover. The Kid threw himself down, hugged the dust. Slugs zipped around him, smacked into wood and dirt. The Kid opened up in retaliation, heard his slugs ricocheting from the rock behind which Grat crouched, heard his slugs go whining away harmlessly into the night.

Frustration blew up inside the Kid. He'd run the man down, take his chance, smoke the skunk out or die trying. He stopped to reload. A slug took his hat. He picked it up, clapped it back on his head.

Grat Boyce stopped shooting. His voice rang out.

'Boys! It's Mal Jackson. He's gone loco. He's a killer. Get him.'

The footsteps rushed then. Too late, the Kid realized his peril. He rose, turning. Something loomed in front of him. Something burst on his head with a blinding flash then, after that, there was only blackness.

When he came to he was lying on a bunk in the bunkhouse, and Jo Lemaine was bending over him. Behind, for now he was never far away, was Henry Grocott. Round about too, were Diamond K boys: pudgy Len Mallin, pint-size Ben Drage; and others. Ben Drage said, 'We're mighty sorry, Mal . . . We took Grat's word. Until Morty told us we . . .'

Morty's voice broke in then, and the Kid was heartened by the sound of it.

'You've got to excuse them, Mal. They've been Grat's saddle-pards for years. They didn't know he'd turned snake.'

The Kid half-rose. Hammers beat at his head.

He forced himself to turn it and saw Morty through a kind of haze. The coloured boy was in the bunk behind him.

'Grat? Where is he?' queried the Kid hoarsely.

'As soon as we downed you he ran,' said Ben Drage. 'He got a horse an' was away before Morty could warn us.'

'Wal, let's . . .' The Kid broke off, clapping his hand to his head. It was festooned with bandages.

'It's all right,' said pudgy Len Mallin. 'You ain't shot. I just laid the barrel o' my gun across the side of your head. I hope you ain't gonna hold it agin me, Mal.'

'No,' grunted the Kid, with a sudden spurt of humour. 'I guess you can't help bein' a natural stinkweed.'

The laughter was strained. The Kid levered himself a little higher. Giant fists tried to beat him down again. The light spun around him. Through gritted teeth he said, 'Wal, what're we waitin' for? Let's get after that skunk!'

'The boys'll catch him and bring him back don't you fret,' said Ben Drage.

Hands pressed against the Kid's shoulders. Not fists this time; and real too, real hands. They pushed him down. He resisted at first but he had to let himself go.

The faces came into focus again. He saw that it

was Jo who had pushed him down. He had been on the verge of cussing but now he choked it back. Henry Grocott was still there, and the rest of them; and now, the wizened face of Hiram Kramer came into view.

'You've got to rest that head a bit, young man, or you're going to be mighty sick. You've just got to let it settle. It'll be all right in a bit.'

Settle, is it, thought the Kid scornfully. His head felt like it was bouncing about up in the rafters, and his body was attached to it by a neck six foot long, six feet of throbbing pain. But he had to admit that the little lawyer's pronouncement was a wise one. He lay still.

The cook came in with coffee and the Kid was able to bring his head down from the rafters and get his lips to a hot steaming cup. He began to feel much better. Over his shoulder, he shot questions at Morty Jaques.

'You very bad, Morty?'

'No. Just a crease in my side. I guess Grat was jest a mite too fast.'

'How come you tumbled to him?'

'My gal, Lindy, works at The Golden Calf. Mahself I hate the place, I don't go there if I can help it. One night when she was slipping out the back way to meet me she saw Grat leaving and Burt Hopson waving him good-bye or somep'n, like they wuz old pals. She told me an' I started to do some investigating on my lonesome. I didn't intend to breathe a word to anybody unless I found out Grat was really four-flushing. After all, on the surface Burt Hopson's allus been friendly with everybody – I thought mebbe Grat was playing Burt at his own game. I've rode with Grat a long time and I jest didn't want to think he was a sidewinder. He must've bin on to me too, but how or when I dunno . . .'

'He acted all above-board to me,' said the Kid. 'If Hopson wanted me out of the way I wonder Grat didn't try an' do the job for him. I guess he had plenty of chances.'

'Mebbe he didn't have the right kind of chances. Mebbe Hopson didn't want him to take chances an' show his hand yet. Grat was pretty well forced to play along with the rest of us . . .'

Morty chuckled, went on: 'When I brought the news in that you were in jail that time, Ma Brannigan conscripted Grat an' some of the boys. The little bushwhack scheme that Hopson an' the sheriff had got worked out for you was a dead flop. I'll bet Grat was scared he'd get shot by one of his new-found friends.'

'That bushwhack fix. That was the way they got my brother, I guess,' said the Kid.

The rest of the folks in the bunkhouse sat and

listened. Their eyes were being opened.

'Yes,' said Morty slowly. 'An' I bin' thinking. When old Luke Price an' some of us boys rode after them rustlers the day Luke was killed Grat Boyce wasn't with us. He was out on the range someplace.'

'That's right shore 'nough,' put in Ben Drage; and one or two of the other boys affirmed this.

'Grat could've bushwhacked ol' Luke and planted Pete's rifle there,' said Morty. 'Unless it was one of Hopson's boys specially detailed for the job.'

'Either way,' said the Kid grimly, 'Grat, Burt Hopson, the sheriff, and all the rest of them are rope-bait. Me, I can't wait that long. Hot lead's quicker.' He swung his feet from the bunk. This time he made it without the roof falling on his head.

'Wait a minute,' said Morty. 'I got sump'n else to tell yuh. I bin out to see my gal, Lindy, tonight . . .'

The Kid didn't say he already knew that; he said, 'Yeh? Had she any news?'

'Yes,' said Morty. 'An' I meant to spout it soon as I'd taken care o' Grat. Things didn't work out quite the way I planned. Anyway, Lindy said that The Golden Calf closed kinda early tonight and the girls were sent home an' told to stay at Tombstone Kate's place. Lindy an' Kate Prather snook out . . .'

The Kid remembered Kate Prather. She was the blonde who had ridden out to him that evening to tell him of Jo's plight.

'. . . They snook along the backs to The Golden Calf. It was all locked up, blinds drawn an' everything but there were lights. They managed to peep through cracks in the blinds and they saw that the place was full o' men. All Hopson's boys and a few more besides. Then others started to come along the street an' the girls had to run for it. They weren't spotted. It looked like Hopson was holdin' a convention or something.'

'Gathering his battalions around him,' said Henry Grocott sonorously.

'That's about it,' agreed the Kid. 'I guess he aims to show his hand all the way purty soon.'

He was sitting on the edge of the bed in his stocking feet. 'We got lookouts?' he asked.

He was assured that they had, that an attacking force would be heard long before they got there, that the Brannigan signal-fire would be spotted immediately if it was lit.

Morty Jaques started to talk again. 'While we're getting the books straight I've jest remembefed sump'n else. Grat Boyce was at The Golden Calf the night Joe Cater was shot. Lindy saw him there.'

'He sure got around,' said the Kid. But his mind

was only half on what Morty had said, and his own reply. What did it matter now who had killed Joe Cater? Joe had been small fry. Grat couldn't die more than once anyway, and he had to die, the Kid was resolved on that. There was going to be a lot of killing. He had thought maybe he had finished with violence. He felt suddenly old beyond his years. He had seen far too much blood and strife. But what could a man do? He braced himself, body and mind. A man just couldn't set an' let things go by. Sometimes a man had to do certain things – just had to. He made a vow. He was a fighting man and fighting men were needed now here, right here. Then afterwards there might be peace. He hoped he might live to see that peace. 'Where's my boots?' he said.

He rose and Jo Lemaine and Henry Grocott both started towards him. But they stopped in their tracks. Mal Jackson was all through being pampered, his cold eyes told them that.

'My gunbelt, too,' he said.

Jo found him his boots, Henry his gunbelt. He fixed himself up. They found his hat too, complete with the bullet-hole in its crown. He tried to put the hat on but it wouldn't stay atop the bandages. The Kid flung the hat disgustedly away from him. Morty grinned at him from the bunk next door.

Then the coloured man's face sobered again.

'Maybe I can . . .' He was struggling upwards as he spoke but fell back with a yelp of pain.

'For Pete's sake,' cried Henry Grocott. 'Do you want to burst that wound open again.'

'Don't you fret, Morty,' said Ben Drage. 'I'll lend you my old buffalo gun. Then if any o' them skunks get this far you'll be able to blow 'em wide open.'

Morty began to grin again.

The Kid said: 'What time is it?'

Henry Grocott took a doeskin pouch from his vest pocket and produced a magnificent gold hunter. 'It's almost three a.m.', he said.

'Well, if they don't come soon dawn will be here before them.'

Then, almost as an echo of the Kid's words, there was a shout from outside. 'Riders comin'.'

'Those five riders who went after Grat,' said Ben Drage. 'They'll be cut off.'

But the approaching riders turned out to be those very five men. All intact, too. The first one bust into the bunkhouse.

'There's a mob riding this way.'

'How about Grat Boyce?' asked the Kid.

'We got him.'

'Where is he?'

'He's outside. He's daid. His hoss must've gone lame or somethin'. He must've been ridin' like a madman. We caught him up sooner'n we expected. I dropped the horse with a shot an' Grat went over its head. He was dead when we got him. Busted neck. We packed him back . . . Hey!' He got all breathless again, 'that mob's comin' fast.'

His voice echoed and died and there was a fraction of stillness. Into it Hiram Kramer dropped a few words. 'So Grat Boyce met a judgement swifter and greater than ours.'

The little man took his huge Frontier-model Colt from somewhere in the recesses of his clothing and began methodically to clean it. Everybody became galvanized as weapons were sought, checked.

'Anybody out at the signal-fire?' shouted the Kid.

'Yes,' said Ben Drage. 'Two men. We can give 'em a call as soon as we want it lit. They'll be able to spot the Brannigan's fire if they light their's too.'

The Kid wondered suddenly if the attackers would split into two sections and attack the Brannigan place too. But wouldn't that be too big a risk – unless Burt Hopson had got heavy reinforcements, professional gunslingers brought in from outside.

Curly Randle and his boys would give a good account of themselves. But say if the mob did break through there, get at Ma Brannigan, Lucy, Betty Lou? His knees went weak as he thought of Betty Lou in the rough and lecherous hands of border carrion . . .

But the hoofbeats were coming nearer now, shaking the ground, and the besieged ranch was getting ready to spout fire.

Jo Lemaine, a rifle in her hand, was marching purposefully towards a window. Both the Kid and Henry made for her at the same time but from different directions.

'Jo,' said Henry. 'This is man's work. You better get back here where . . .'

'What do you take me for?' Her lips curled. 'I can shoot. I'll wager I'm a better shot than some of the men here.'

Over her head Henry exchanged glances with the Kid, who shrugged. Jo continued on her way, reached the window, went down on one knee before it.

'They're hunting cover,' yelled a man. 'Don't let 'em find any.'

'They'll have a job,' chuckled pudgy Len Marrin. 'We shifted it all.'

Ben Drage ran to the back door and shouted, 'Light the fire!'

There was an answering cry. Then the shooting started.

Slugs thunked into the heavy log walls of the bunkhouse without penetrating them. Old Luke Price, though he'd had the reputation of a skinflint, hadn't believed in half-measures. Other ranchers could build their ranches of clapboard but nothing but logs would serve for him, and the thicker the better.

A slug came through a window, buzzed across the room and buried itself in the opposite wall. There hadn't been anybody in the line of fire. Everybody was in cover. Even Morty Jaques had been carried from his bunk to another one in shelter and near a window. He had Ben Drage's buffalo gun too.

A little later the Kid heard the unmistakable boom of the Sharps and turned his head. Morty had managed to get out of the bunk and was at the window, firing coolly and methodically.

The Kid turned back to his own shooting. Out there in the darkness the figures of his enemies were pretty nebulous. As far as he could judge, he had downed two of 'em so far. Some of them hugged meagre cover, others remained on their horses and made little skirmishing rushes from each flank. Each time they were driven back. So far none of the defenders entrenched in the stout bunkhouse had been hit.

But then the first tragedy happened.

Lawyer Kramer gave a gasping cry and flopped over on his back. He was dead before they got to him.

'I guess he would've wanted it that way,' said Henry Grocott. 'He proved himself a real Western character after all. We'll all remember him and the way he fought for right in the end. He'll like that.'

He covered the small body reverently with a blanket. The attackers opened up again with a vengeance. Those of the defenders who had run to Hiram sought cover again. Another man was hit, spinning to the floor with a bullet in his shoulder. Jo was soon at his side with whisky and bandages to give him temporary succour.

Ben Drage crawled to the Kid's side. 'Some of those skunks have reached the ranchhouse an' the barn,' he said.

'I was wondering all along whether we ought to put men there,' said the Kid. 'But I figured that the bunkhouse was right opposite the rise which that mob would be bound to use an' it might lessen our power as a fighting force if we got spread out too much. As we are now they can't split us up.'

'You're right there,' said Ben Drage. 'We did the best thing I think; they're gettin' cut down quicker than we are. While we hold 'em off Curly

Randle an' his boys'll be on their way here. Things'll be more even when they get here.'

But the Kid, who had probably seen more fighting than the older man was not over-optimistic. 'I hope Curly'll hurry then,' he said. 'Those skunks are pressing hard. There are some real picked marksmen out there an' things are beginning to get real hot.'

'How about those boys?' said Ben. 'The boys at the fire. They'll be cut off.'

'Hell, why didn't they run in while they had a chance?'

'I guess maybe they thought they'd keep the fire goin'. We didn't want it to fizzle out before they spotted it at the Brannigan place did we?'

'No, that's for sure,' agreed the Kid, now ashamed of his bad temper. He took it out on a rider who was charging recklessly towards the bunkhouse. The man went backwards over his horse's tail. The beast wheeled and galloped back the way it had come. The man lay still.

'Let's go get those two boys.' said the Kid.

Finally Len Mallin and Henry Grocott came too, darting after Ben and the Kid to the back door. They ducked out, one by one.

The fire blazed gloriously, throwing a lurid glow for yards around it. The two boys were making a run for it but a couple of horsemen rode to intercept them. The Kid and his companions started shooting.

A horse screamed with pain and flopped down, throwing its rider clear. The other horseman turned tail. A shot from Henry Grocott took his hat off, then he disappeared into the night. The fallen man rose and started to run. The Kid caught him up, dodged a vicious blow. He tripped the man up and stunned him with a smashing blow from his gun-barrel. A slug plucked at his pants. Somebody was potting at him from the shelter of the ranch house. He ran for the veranda, knowing his three companions were close behind.

Another slug plucked at the bandages on his head and he realized the whiteness there was a good target. Behind him somebody let out a high gasping cry. Then he hit the veranda and rolled into cover. Henry and Ben joined him. Len Mallin lay still out there in the dust.

'He's dead,' said Ben. 'The slug hit him plumb in the throat.'

The Kid kicked open the back door of the ranch house and they dived in. The three bushwhackers, who had been entrenched in one of the back rooms, now ran out into the passage. Things were mighty confused for a moment. There was a lot of shooting. Ben Drage went down with a bullet in his leg. The Kid cursed as a slug creased his arm, he was glad it was his left one. He cut down the man in front of him and then there was only one man left for Ben had already put paid to the other, who lay moaning feebly in a corner.

In the gun-flashes the Kid had seen the face of the third man, the staring, mouthing face of Sheriff George Corletta.

Henry Grocott's gun spoke heavily from beside the Kid. The sheriff screamed shrilly. They heard him fall. When they reached him he was dead.

Between them, Henry and the Kid helped Ben out onto the veranda. Out front the shooting was reaching a crescendo. There was a lull and the sound of voices shouting.

'I suttinly hope that's our own folks,' groaned Ben Drage.

Hoofs thundered. Two riders passed across the glow the fire.

'Get 'em!' howled Ben.

His two companions lowered him and started shooting. One man disappeared into the night but the other man's horse was shot from under him. He rose and began to run.

'It's Hopson.' said Ben Drage.

'He's mine,' said the Kid softly and jumped from the veranda.

Hopson saw him coming and turned at bay.

There by the fire, as the distance lessened between the two men, it was bright as day. The firelight was like the glow of a blood-red sun.

Hopson's first shot missed the Kid entirely. His second plucked at the Kid's shoulder. Hopson fired again, savagely, his eyes glowing in the firelight. His world had disintegrated around him, and he was losing his cold gambler's nerve. It was proved now if it had never been proved before, that when the old plainsmen said the man who shot fastest didn't hit the most turkeys they were spreading words of wisdom.

Hopson's third shot missed too. Hopson screamed curses, steadied his gun with both hands. The Kid's first shot came then. The slug slammed into Hopson's shoulder, spinning him around.

The Kid held his gun out in front of him and fired as if he was shooting at a fairground target. There was no expression on his face at all and his eyes in the firelight were like red marbles. His second shot beat into Hopson's chest, slamming him back into the fire. He didn't feel the flames. He was already dead.

The Kid holstered his gun, went back and helped Henry to get Ben into the bunkhouse.

The battle was over. Curly Randle and his boys had arrived and congratulations were being exchanged all round. Prisoners were lined up. Henry joined Jo again as she succoured the wounded, irrespective of which side they belonged to. The big lawyer and the shapely dark girl worked side by side and it was obvious to everybody present that they aimed to stay that way.

Then Ma Brannigan turned up and Lucy and the kids and Betty Lou. The Kid looked at Betty Lou. She looked at him. They didn't have to touch each other.

'Well, sis,' said the Kid. 'Do you think you could clean this place up well enough to live in?'

'I think so,' said Lucy. 'If you'll stay here and help me to run it.'

The Kid looked at Betty Lou again. She moved then, put her hand in his.

He grinned at Lucy. 'I guess I'll stay,' he said.